THE MAGIC—

From a giant wishing ring to a flying carpet, an island of no return, and a wicked wizard's spell . . .

THE MENACE—

From a kingdom's darkest dungeons and the Galumphing Beast to a two-headed ogre and the doom of the Topless Tower, all of which had proved the ultimate challenges of many a hero's life . . .

AND THE MADCAP ADVENTURERS—

From the stalwart knight Mandricardo and his bold Amazonian lady love Callipygia to Braggadochio and Sir Blundamore and their amazing tales of rampage and rescues in Terra Magica, that incredible realm where anything could happen and it usually did!

Author's Note

This tale is laid in Terra Magica, the world next to our own, and as close to ours as are two pages in a book ... so very close, in fact, that our most sensitive poets and artists and tellers-of-tales and dreamers have glimpsed something of its history and geography and zoology, which they have recorded in our myths and legends, travelers' tales and bestiaries and fairy-stories.

The time of this story is the twilight of the Golden Age.

CALLIPYGIA
LIN CARTER

Further Adventures in Terra Magica

DAW BOOKS, INC.

DONALD A. WOLLHEIM, PUBLISHER

DAW Book Collectors No. 736.

First Printing, February 1988

2   3   4   5   6   7   8   9

PRINTED IN CANADA
COVER PRINTED IN THE U.S.A.

This one is for Betsy and Peter,
and in particular for little Zoë Alexandra,
who is much too young to read it.

CONTENTS

BOOK FIVE   The secret of the Ring

BOOK ONE

Trouble in Taprobane

1

Consequences of Getting Caught in the Rain

Now, it was getting rather well along into midafternoon there on the broad and grassy plains of Pontus near the shores of the Euxine Sea, when a sizable party came riding due east, toward the river Thermodon, whose broad and glistening floods formed the border between this country—it was the famous country of the Amazons, I will have you know—and the next, of whose name I am not at all certain, not that it matters in the least, since whatever country it was, it does not at all enter into our story. But where was I?

Oh, yes—they came riding at a moderate pace, rather slower than they would ordinarily have ridden, but that was because of the mule. Her name was Minerva, and she served the two main riders—for the rest of them were a sort of honor guard, or escort, you might say—served them, I was saying, as their packmule, and carried their luggage, including a picnic hamper liberally stocked with food and drink, a parting gift from the palace

cook, who had rather taken a fancy to Sir Mandricardo.

That is him, Mandricardo, I mean, riding in
front, next to the rather plump young woman in
the Amazonian armor (what there was of it, and
there was not very much, for, while certainly not
immodest, the Amazons tend rather to be con-
temptuous of wearing too much armor, priding
themselves on their martial spirit and womanly
courage.

Now this Mandricardo was the son of King
Agricane of Tartary—no, neither the Mandricardo
nor the Agricane in your *Song of Roland*, but de-
scendants of theirs, both Mandricardo and Agricane
being in the manner of family names—and a famous knight-errant, our Mandricardo, whose exploits are celebrated in a work entitled the *Chronicle
Narrative of the Deeds of Mandricardo of Tartary*,
from which this book of mine is taken.

He was tall, with broad shoulders and long legs,
of swarthy complexion, being a Tartar, with dark
eyes, drooping mustaches and an aquiline nose
which had been broken once, or, it may be, twice,
and had been set rather askew, giving him a slightly
rakish look to his features. He wore plate armor,
and had a lot of lion-skins knotted together and
slung about his shoulders, after the fashion cur-
rently popular in Tartary.

You may be wondering what on earth a Tartar
was doing riding about on the verdant plains of
Amazonia, but the answer lies in the robust young
person riding at his left hand; this was Callipygia,
one of the seventeen daughters of the Queen of
the Amazons, and Mandricardo's betrothed. He
and his lady-love were presently engaged on riding the width of the world: they had begun in

the gloomy pine forests of the Kingdom of the
Franks, in the world's west, and were *en route* to
Tartary, Sir Mandricardo's homeland, which is
about as far east as you can possibly go without
either riding into the waters of the Unknown Sea,
or falling off the Edge of the World.* To be a bit
more precise, it is right next door to China, where
the son of the famous Emperor Aladdin rules,
and just a shade north of the Empire of Prester
John.

Callipygia had long hair blowing behind her in
the breeze, and a long spear, a small round sort of
shield called a *targe*, a bow and a quiver of
arrows—your Amazon, you know, is famous for
her archery—and some bits of burnished steel
armor. That is, a breastplate, greaves to guard her
shins, a mail-skirt like a short kilt, made of leather
straps studded with disks of steel and silver-gilt,
gauntlets, a stout girdle, and so on. Oh, yes, upon
her upper left forearm she wore a peculiar bronze
ring with uncouth markings upon it in *an unknown
tongue*.

She was mounted on a handsome roan mare
named Blondel, while Sir Mandricardo rode astride
a magnificent black charger whom he called
Bayardetto. And you have already been introduced
to Miranda.

For the past two weeks, Mandricardo had been an
honored guest at the court of Queen Megamastaia
in her splendid capital of Themiscyra (or at least it
is by that name that the historian Herodotus re-

---

* Just a word here to remind my reader that our scene is not laid
in Terra Cognita—the Lands We Know—but in Terra Magica.
And I am fairly certain that Terra Magica is flat, and has a real
Edge; all of the better-thought-of authorities agree on this point,
so who am I to question it?

fers to it, and he knows much more about these matters than I do, certainly): but now they were on their way, as I have already explained, to Tartary.

Sixteen well-mounted young Amazon women rode with them, as an honor guard or whatever, escorting them at least as far as the border, where they intended to ford the shallow floods of the river Thermodon and continue on into the east.

These young women were, as you might have expected, the sisters of Dame Callipygia, and as they rode along they were chattering away to each other (but mostly to Callipygia) like a flock of magpies. Sisters tend to be chatty in Amazonia as elsewhere, I have found.

"I say, Cally, you will write home, won't you, when you get to Tartary, and tell us all about the wedding and what it's like there, and so forth— you know," said a splendid tall girl with red hair and green eyes and freckles.

"Well, I will try to, dear," said Callipygia. "But, Antiope, I have no way of knowing what the postal system is like in Tartary, and *you* know how unreliable the mail service is hereabouts—"

"Oh, but Cally, you must tell us about the wedding!" cried another, a fair-skinned maid with shining black tresses and huge dark eyes.

"As I say, I'll certainly *try*, Penthesileia—"

"Oh, and Sir Mandricardo, when the baby is born—well, don't *blush* so, there's *bound* to be a *baby*, isn't there?—couldn't you get the court painter of Tartary to do a nice miniature to send us, so we'll know what the little darling looks like, and which one of you it takes after?" This request came from a striking blonde girl with a lovely golden tan and clear blue eyes; her name was Hippolyta, and by now it must be as obvious as the nose on your face that the seventeen daughters of the Amazonian Queen were each fathered by a different husband. Such was, in fact, the case, for Amazonian Queens do not marry for life, you know, but only for the season. It makes for variety, as Megamastaia always said.

"Oh, here now, dash it all, Hippolyta, what," said Mandricardo helplessly, crimson to the tips of his ears. "Dashed rot you're talking, gel . . . haven't even had the dashed weddin' yet, Cally, and these dashed sisters of yours are anticipatin' *babies* and all, I say! Rawther a bit much, what?"

And the sixteen young women giggled at his discomforture and exchanged whispered comments, one to the other.

"Now, now, girls, stop teasing Mandricardo, do," laughed Callipygia indulgently. They were, just then, passing a dilapidated stone monument, much overgrown with weeds, which marked the site of a battle famous in the history of Amazonia; it commemorated a former incursion into Lycia, when the Amazonian army had invaded that realm but had been so gloriously defeated by the celebrated hero Bellerophon that the Amazons, ever eager to recognize valor, even in their foes, had erected (by popular subscription) the monument to commemorate his prowess. Real sports, those Amazons . . .

But another of Callipygia's numerous sisters was speaking: a platinum blonde with ripe curves and striking amethystine eyes, and Cally was just answering her question. "Yes, Kaydesa, dear, I expect that Mandricardo and I will be able to visit on vacation at least once a year—don't you think we can, Mandro?—because, after all, we have the Magic Flying Carpet that Mandro purloined from that wicked magician, and a Magic Carpet *does* so help one to get around more swiftly and easily than on horseback—"

"Looks like we're in for a spot of rain," remarked another girl with auburn, wavy hair and big brown eyes. Her name was Radigund. They glanced aloft, to see that her observation seemed quite accurate. The day had been bright and sunny and clear when they had set out from the gates of Themiscyra that morning, but now it was definitely clouding up and a pall of shadow lay over the lush green plain and the edge of the wind had that damp excitement that foreshadows a coming storm.

Yes, even as they looked, there was a grumble above them in the dark-bellied clouds, that sort of digestive noise that thunder makes, and they winced at the uncanny flicker of lightning.

By this time large fat droplets had begun to come splattering down, and this was annoying, since all of the riders were armed and you know how awfully steel rusts in the rain, of course, but it was particularly annoying to Sir Mandricardo. During his recent travels and adventures across the broad face of Terra Magica he simply had not been able to find the time in his busy schedule of confronting giants and witches and genies and dragons and pirates and enchanters and so on and so forth, to keep his armor quite as oiled and cleaned and polished as he would ordinarily have done. Indeed, one of the reasons he had lingered so long in Themiscyra, enjoying the lavish hospi-

tality of Queen Megamastaia, was so that the royal
armorer could give his suit a good going over,
tightening the rivets and scouring and oiling and
polishing and whatever . . . and now he was about
to get drenched in what looked to be a veritable
downpour.

"Oh, I say, dash it all!" he growled disgustedly.
"Filthy luck, what?"

"Girls, it looks like a real deluge coming," said
Callipygia. "Mandro and I will take shelter under
those trees over there, but there doesn't look
like there's room enough for all of you, so why
don't you head back home? Thanks for escorting
us, but I know the way from here, and with the
least little bit of luck you can all get back in-
doors before the rain begins really falling hard,
and I know poor Penthesileia *just* had her hair
done . . . ?"

The sixteen sisters quickly agreed this was the
wisest thing to do, and each gave Callipygia and
her betrothed a good-bye kiss and a hug, and
before very much longer, the troop of young Amazons turned about and went galloping back across
the plains to where the towers and ramparts of
Themiscyra gleamed in the distance; as they rode,
waving their spears like so many Valkyries in a
production of *Die Walkure*, they shrilled their famous Amazon war-cries to the welkin, whatever
that is, and these ringing cries of, "Yoicks! Yoicks!
Tally-ho! Hark-forrard!"—the which had oft, ere
this, struck terror into the hearts of their foemen
on many a famous field—sounded eerily over the
broad plain under the lowering sky.

"Fine gels, those sisters of yours, m'love," grinned
Mandricardo. "Have to invite the whole family out
to Tartary, what, to the christenin'."

"*What* christening?" demanded Callipygia, blushing violently, "we haven't even had the honeymoon yet, you great lout!"

He chuckled, and they headed toward the distant stand of trees, as the raindrops were pelting down by now, fat and heavy.

The trees, oddly enough, were not at all the sort of trees that grew in these parts of Terra Magica (as a matter of fact, there were remarkably few trees that grew at all on the grassy plains of Amazonia, which more or less explains why they had grassy plains, instead of mighty forests. They were, I say, oddly enough, chestnuts and oaks and beech and Australian pines* and teakwood and bamboo and baobabs and, well, I-don't-know-what-all, but I *distinctly remember seeing* the sort of date palms they have growing in desert oases (or do I mean *oasi*?), and apple trees, a lime tree in full bloom, and several tropicalish-looking things that might have been mango and guava trees, not to mention tall banana stalks.

However, this unusual mixture of vegetation was far—I might even say *very* far—from being the most peculiar thing about that clump of thickly-grown trees that grew there on the green verdant plains of Amazonia, near the gliding silver floods of the mighty Thermodon.

For not more than three minutes after Mandricardo and his lady-love and their animals entered the little grove, vanishing from our view, the whole dashed great clump of trees (as the Tartar knight

---

*Yes, yes, *I* know: never mind that Australia hadn't even been discovered yet; just sit back and enjoy the story, won't you, and stop picking flaws in it.

would probably say) picked itself up and flew away, soon dwindling to a green mote in the distance, traveling at a fairly good clip in the general direction of Hindoostan.

2

The Gentleman with the Walrus Mustache

The two wasted no time in seeking shelter from the storm, and got out of the saddle and under the thickest foliage they could find, while Mandricardo fussed and fretted, dabbing rain-spots from his gleaming suit of armor. Callipygia stared thoughtfully around with a puzzled expression on her face, noticing the ilex bushes (which grow on the parched plains of Persia), clumps of hibiscus from South America, boxwood shrubs from the northern countries, blackberry bushes, rhododendrons from Southeast Asia ... which were growing in between orange trees and banyans, palms and pines, birch, teak, and ... well, you get the idea.

Shortly thereafter, and before she had a chance to mention the strange mixed nature of the trees and bushes, there came distantly to their ears the sound of someone singing, if that is quite the word I want. The voice made up in vigor what it lacked in pitch, and the song was none other than

"*Scots wha hae wi' Wallace bled,*" and never you mind writing to me and pointing out that this is an anachronism.*

Mandricardo looked at Callipygia, and Callipygia looked at Mandricardo. They loosened their swords in their scabbards, except that, come to think of it, Callipygia didn't have a sword, having misplaced it somewhere along the way, so she just sort of hefted her spear. And they headed through the swishing bushes, paying no heed to the wet slap of the leaves against them, and Mandricardo clanked down his visor . . . then, as he took a good look at the spectacle before him, he clicked it up again and stared in amazement.

Before them on the edge of a little pond was one of those folding lawn chairs of wooden slats and painted canvas, you know the kind. Seated therein was a long-legged individual clad only in a suit of long red woolen underwear with a buttoned drop-seat. He also wore a green celluloid eyeshade like *croupiers* wear in gambling casinos, and a pair of dilapidated, well-worn carpet slippers. He was dividing his attention in about equal thirds between refreshing himself with long, glugging swigs from a fat little jug of black glass, taking deep puffs from a battered briar pipe whose capacious bowl seemed stuffed with some noxious, some *downright poisonous* smelling shredded weed (from whose nasty stench the smoldering stuff could well have been employed in fending off ravenous mosquitoes, and, come to think of it, there wasn't a single mosquito in sight), and, de-

* I've had occasion to remark on this point to you before. While I don't want to seem overly stern, I must say I don't want to have to mention this matter again.

voted the last third of his attention, now that his song was over, to his regular afternoon pastime of cheating himself at solitaire. This he accomplished by means of a greasy pack of well-thumbed playing cards which he slapped down on the back of his shield, which was spread across his lap. A heap of dented, rusty armor stood under a nearby tree.

Cannily noticing the arrival of company, he bent upon the twain a twinkling, shrewd, humorous blue eye (never mind the fact that the whites were rather bloodshot), and, politely tipping his eyeshade in Callipygia's direction, gave them an amiable wink. He had a bony red face, whose ruddy cheeks and purplish bulb of a nose were tastefully adorned with burst capillaries, a long jaw and a bristly red mustache of the kind which Providence generally reserves for British sergeant-majors and the bull-walrus. Removing his smoldering briar, he summoned up his internal capacities, spat resoundingly into a steel pot by his side (which they later discovered to be his helmet), thereby preparing to exercise his considerable powers of elocution, and hailed the newcomers with affable hospitality.

"And a fine gude mornin' to ye both, sor and moddom; aye, a braw lovely day the noo, beyond a doot, now that a bit of rain has passed us by, ye'll ken. Pray step into me parlor, so to speak, and mak' yereselves to hame. I'm no' a drinking mon, thank losh, excepting noo and then, and puirly on the advice of me physician, ye'll onderstond, so I'm afeared I canna offer ye a gert voriety of refroshments, but if ye care the noo, I ha' me ain tipple ... a sovereign remedy for the rheumatiz, the sciaticks, cheelbains, too, an' mony another complain of man and beest, so porhops ye'll deign to join me in just a dollop of this excelint specific an' panacear?"

And, politely wiping dry the jug's mouth on the sleeve of his long woolen underwear, he proffered the fat jug of thick black glass to Mandricardo, who accepted it dazedly and lifted it to his lips. It glugged for a time, and when the Tartar knight lowered the black jug again, Callipygia watched his swarthy features first pale to the sickly hue of spoiled milk, then become a rich royal purple. Tears welled uncontrollably in his eyes; he swallowed painfully, then drew a long, ragged breath, and when he exhaled, an astringent aroma was added to the air. It was alcohol, but like nothing Callipygia had yet smelled.

"What . . . *was* . . . that?" wheezed Mandricardo a bit later. The man with the walrus mustache smiled a proudly bashful smile, even though that may sound like a contradiction.

"A beverage common to distant Caledonia, gude sor, and far, far fra' hame here amongst the feelthy heathen (and beggin' yere pardon, moddom, on the chance ye be a native to these parts . . . a braw lovely country hereaboots!); but, returning to yere question, me gude sor, 'tis a refreshing and health-restoring beverage distilled fra' grain by a meesteerious process known only to the Caledonians. Well, I'll join ye then in a dollop meself, to keep ye company, as 'twere, and to fortify me constitution against the treacherous miasmas whereweeth the region aboonds. . . ." He lifted the half-gallon jug to his lips, drank long and gluggily, and when he lowered it again, surely

it was but a pint. "Ahhh!" he exhaled with satisfaction, his breath knocking a wasp out of the
air in midflight. He wiped his bristly mustache,
wringing the last drop from its fringes, the which
he pensively sucked from his fingertip. "Ah, ye
were askin' whut the sagacious vintners o' far Caledonia hae named the beverage . . . 'tis called
usquebae."

Now that his tonsils had recovered from their
momentary spasms of panic, caused by the first
swallow of the contents of the black jug, and
Mandricardo's throat lining seemed no longer as
raw and scorched as it had a moment or two
before, he was aware of a not-unpleasant glow
blossoming in his stomach, and a soothing warmth
spread rapidly through his veins. Absently, he
reached for the jug again, half-lifted it to his lips,
then politely paused in inquiry.

"Dashed jug can't hold much more, old chap.
Sure it's all tickety-boo with you if I try another
draught?"

"Haw, haw," brayed the other, nodding his head
affably, and falling out of his lawn chair without
bothering to get up again, "do pray help yeresel'
. . . 'tis a braw lovely *bottomless jug* I ha' here, the
geeft o' a frondly enchanter, I ken me his name
was Busyrane . . . and 'twull sairve to fortify all
our constitutions against this dommed onhealthy
climate . . ." He fell to humming "*Scots wha' hae*"
under his breath again, while lurching unsteadily
to his feet; he stood there, wobbling a little in the
knees, clutching the back of his lawn chair for
support, while muttering something about "treech-
erous unsteady land underfoot, a *jefinite treemor*,
there, did ye not feel it the noo, sor?"

Callipygia stepped forward and helped their host back into his rickety chair, since Mandricardo was, just then, leaning against a banyan tree and mumbling something about "earthquakes" under his breath.

"Ah, me thonks, gude moddom, I'm afeared the state of me health is nain to gude these days . . . and what a theerst these dommed feelthy southern climes do gi' a mon! I'll thonk ye to pass me jug back, sor:" the jug was upended again and the Amazon girl watched with wonderment as the rather large and knobbly adam's apple in the drinker's scraggly throat jerked and jiggled in time to his swallowings. A musical crash sounded from behind her as Mandricardo fell over.

She went over to help prop her man against a tree with his back securely wedged into place. "I say, old gel, *is* it an earthquake? Bally wood seems to be flying—there goes a cloud zipping by now, dashed if it didn't—"

"We've been flying for some little time, but you got too drunk to notice," she commented acidly.

He was not too inebriated to feel a pang of dismay.

"Oh, I say! Don't tell me we're trapped in that filthy Wandering Garden that enchantress-blighter, what-zer-name—?

"Acrasia," the Amazon supplied.

"—Acrasia—built to trap wandering knights and heroes into her lustful embrace, what?" he finished, and all in one breath, too.

"Quite," she said succinctly. She was trying to get his helmet off, having already unbuckled and removed his gauntlets.

"Yus, 'tis vurra, vurra true," remarked the man in the lawn chair (they *still* had not gotten around to introducing themselves to each other, but I am getting tired of referring to Braggadocio as "the man with the walrus mustache" or "the man in the lawn chair" and so on, so you might as well know right now that his name was Braggadocio, and he was not the one in *The Faerie Queene*, either).

"Ye've a pairfect richt to feel dismay, me gude sor an' moddom, for, oh, gude losh, I hae' been tropped in this flyin' isle, for weeks an' weeks, whurra, while it gaes gollivonting aroond the londscape like some dommed birdie, and by the noo I'm sick of the whole sorra business! 'Tis a dommed wearisome postime to gae flying aboot like this, far fra' hame, and, onteel the twa' of ye arrived to gie me the pleasure o' yere company, I ha' been alone . . . *alone*. . . ."

The thought of his recent solitary state seemed to touch Sir Braggadocio deeply. His long face became even longer and his expression solemn. ". . . *Alone* . . ." he whispered again to himself in choked tones, chewing morosely on the fringes of his walrus mustache while a salty tear formed in one sad eye. Detaching itself from his eyelash, it trickled down his leathery cheek and splashed neatly into the mouth of the black bottomless jug. "*Alone*," he groaned hollowly again, carefully shifting the receptacle out of line in order to preclude any further undesired lachrymal dilution of its precious contents. And one last time, "*Alone*. . . !"

"Well, you're not alone anymore," said Callipygia briskly. She had by now gotten off the Tartar knight's spiked helmet, but as she turned to speak these comforting words to Braggadocio, he fell over again with another jingling, musical crash, Mandricardo that is, and the Amazon girl disgustedly decided to leave him where he lay, snoring gently.

"What *you* need is some solid food in you!" she snapped at her slumbering lover, and went to unload the picnic basket from the back of Minerva the mule, who was placidly cropping the lush, dewy sward.

Cold water splashed in Mandricardo's face revived him somewhat, and the sight of the sumptuous repast which Callipygia unpacked and laid out on a clean white tablecloth which she spread out on the grass awakened a dormant appetite. The thought of a civilized meal also galvanized Braggadocio into action, for, as he made mournfully plain to his two visitors, all the Wandering Garden had by way of groceries was a huge variety of fruit, from tropical delicacies such as yams, pawpaws, guavas, bananas, coconuts, breadfruit, mangoes and avocado pears, to such fruits of the desert regions as figs, dates, olives, oranges and peaches, while the northern parts of the world supplied walnuts, apples, pears, blueberries, and so on . . . "and a mon gits dommed sick an' tired of eating *fruit* three dommed times a day!" growled the marooned knight (if knight is what he actually was: but here I anticipate).

When the Queen of the Amazons packed a picnic lunch, well, she packed a *LUNCH*. There was a whole broiled chicken with chestnut stuffing and cranberry sauce and celery stuffed with melted cheese and an excellent can or two of paté. There were also green olives stuffed with red pimento, potato salad, candied watermelon rind, smoked oysters and baked sweet potatoes glazed with honey. There were even black Spanish olives, already pitted, and caviar in tins, and kosher deli pickles and a huge slab of succulent Stilton cheese. To wash this down there were bottles of the red wine of Schiraz and of the white wine of Kirmische, half a case of a rather decent champagne, and even a thermos of ice-cold lemonade, for those who preferred a lighter beverage with their lunch.

Few of my readers will have had the rare opportunity to sit on the grass under a flowering acacia tree and eat a superb picnic lunch, while flying across Asia at about seventeen hundred feet, but I assure you, if the occasion ever does happen to come your way, don't let it pass you by.

Mandricardo did not for some reason care to join his lady-love in sampling the excellent white wine his future mother-in-law had chosen from her capacious cellars, saying feebly that his stomach felt oddly queasy just then, but he sipped at the cold lemonade gratefully. Braggadocio had nothing but an utter contempt for such "dommed inseepid pap" as lemonade, and shuddered away from wine, saying that he had an uncle once who swore by a good bottle or two of port every day, and perished miserably of cirrhosis of the liver, that dreadful Scourge of wine-drinkers. No, as he put it staunchly:

"I ha' me ain, thonk ye kindly, and a mon shud stick wi' wha' he knows best, beyond a doot . . . ah, deary me, this eating 'tis a dry and theersty work," and he paused, while demolishing a plump, juicy

drumstick, to guzzle from the potent contents of
the bottomless black jug.

They passed the length of Hindoostan; just at
that moment they were floating over the famous
gardens of the Cachemir; erelong the Sacred River
hove into view, gleaming like burnished copper in
the afternoon light; they soared above the celebrated kingdom of the Gargarids, and flew on
into the unknown south.

3

A Picnic in the Clouds

While they flew, they conversed around mouth-fuls of luncheon and swallows of (a) white wine, (b) lemonade, and (C) *usquebae*. It was at this time that Mandricardo and Callipygia finally got around to introducing themselves to Braggadocio, or "Sir Braggadocio," as he claimed, although the Tartar knight, now much soberer than earlier, looked a bit askance at this. And Callipygia explained to their new friend that they had encountered the Wandering Garden before, during the course of a previous adventure. The other brightened visibly at this, for no matter how he had wracked his brains he had been unable to puzzle his way out of this magical trap set generations before their time by the lustful Acrasia: as Braggadocio phrased it, with his inimitable powers of elocution, "ye can walk into the dommed place like any dommed fool fly into a spidey web, but ye canna walk *owt* ... I ha' tried an' tried 'till me nairves are all a-joomp and a-jangle, but I dinna ken the trick o' it—"

"The way out is to go straight up," said Callipygia a trifle shortly. She happened to be sitting down-wind of Braggadocio and so received the full import of his *usquebae*-laden breath. While she had to admit there were certain benefits from having a picnic with someone whose breath was powerful enough to paralyze any bothersome ants up to some twenty paces away, still, she couldn't help wishing the wind would change.

Those canny, twinkling, and somewhat blood-shot blue eyes twinkled shrewdly at her.

"And joost how, me gude moddom, do ye plan to accoompleesh sich a feat?" he inquired loftily, wrinkling his eyes at the corners and in every way suggesting a man who had just launched a final and devastating shaft of pure logic to demolish the argument of an opponent.

"Oh, we have a Magic Flying Carpet," she said offhandedly.

His face fell; so, as a matter of fact, did the rest of him, and it was fortunate for Braggadocio that he was seated on soft grass and not at a hard table, or he could easily have dealt himself a nasty blow on the point of his jaw.

Callipygia explained how the Carpet's many interesting and utile properties included the ability to expand to virtually any size, in order to accommodate parties large and small. This would come in handy later on, she assumed, but for the moment they must wait for the Garden to settle to earth of its own accord, which it did at some unguessable and Gardenly caprice of its own, from time to time, before they would try leaving it by Carpet-back. She pointed at the opening in the trees which were thickly interlaced over their heads, and open to the sky only above the little pool.

"That opening is not big enough for more than one or two of us to fly out of here at a time, and then there are the horses and the mule, and I see you have a horse, too," she said, kindly including under the same general heading as fitted her superb mare, Blondel, and Mandricardo's magnificent coal-black stallion, the spavined and scrawny nag of Braggadocio's which was tethered across the little clearing around the pool, disinterestedly munching the damp grass and eyeing the other two horses with mild equine curiosity.

Their meal concluded, Callipygia and the Tartar knight sat back against the tree trunks, enjoying the blissful cool of early evening, while Braggadocio entertained them with a modest account of himself and his famous career of knight-errantry. The reason they had not heard of him, he claimed (with an artful pretense of surprise when they informed him that they had not) was obviously that he had wandered into Fairyland quite some years ago, where most of his adventures had occurred, including his famous battle with the ferocious giantess, Eriphilia, whom he slew after heroic exertions and at the conclusion of a nonstop duel that lasted three days and two nights.

Pausing frequently to restore his tissues and to fortify his system against the dangerous humors of these fever-ridden climes, and puffing from time to time upon his filthy briar, he also regaled them with a blow-by-blow account of his duel to the death with the celebrated Saracen chevalier, Sans Foy, and, recalling hazily to mind that Mandricardo, here, was of the Tartar persuasion, he gave his audience a vigorous and colorful account of his various heroic deeds and exploits at

the Siege of Albracca during the war between the
Emperor of Tartary and the Grand Cham, during
which conflict he fought on the Tartar side, beside the gallant Rinaldo himself, whose life he was
fortunate enough to be able to save on three sepa-
rate occasions.

Experiencing in time a certain dryness of throat
from all this talking, he paused to restore his
tissues by a prolonged bout of swigging from the
upended jug, and under the cover of this *glug-
glug-glugging* the Amazon girl inquired in a tactful
whisper if Mandricardo thought there was any
truth to all of this.

"Good gad, no!" he chuckled. "The siege of
Albracca was generations ago, and although I've
heard that mortals don't age at all in Fairyland,
what, I doubt the whole dashed thing."

"What about the duel with Sans Foy? I've *heard*
of Sans Foy."

"Everybody's heard of Sans Foy, m'love: he's in
the jolly old history books, you know! But it was
St. George who fought him."

"And the giantess Eriphilia?"

"Rogero, the Paynim knight, battled against her,
the same Rogero who later became King of the
Bulgars."

"It's all just empty bragging, then?"

Mandricardo chuckled. "I suppose so, old gel.
It's not for nothing he has a bally name like
'Braggadocio'!"

Having finished his imbibement at length, Braggadocio paused for a much needed breath, yawned
jaw-crackingly, and, having audibly collected his
liquid resources, expectorated ringingly into the
helmet which he employed in lieu of a spitoon. He
stretched and yawned another yawn.

"A-weel, I'm for me bed, and, sor and moddom,
I'll bid ye a gude nicht, a vurra gude nicht. It hae
been a braw lovely time the noo, but tomorra's
anither joost as braw, nae doot . . ."

And rising unsteadily to his feet, he gave them a
courtly bow which nearly precipitated him nose-
first into the ground; but, at the last possible moment, and in seeming defiance of the Law of
Gravity, he jerkily maintained his balance and rose
to his full six feet. As the sun had gone down an
hour before, he no longer had need of his eyeshade, so he removed it with a flourish and hung
it on a hook that wasn't there. Giving the offending article of headgear a frosty glare of stern
reproof, he said, "Oh, vurra well, then, domm ye,
lie there on the floor and be dommed to ye!"

He then headed for his hammock, which hung
between the trees just within the edges of the little
wood that grew around the pool. The Tartar and
the Amazon watched him with awe. Considering
the sheer amount of the sulfurous *usquebae* he
had taken aboard, it was more than a little surprising that he could even stand up, much less walk at
all. But he proceeded at a steady pace, although it
was marked that his progress was a trifle erratic,
given to unpredictable swoops and surges, as well
as a decided tendency to yaw to port. However he
reached the hammock, kicked off his slippers, expectorated one last time into the bushes, and fell
into the swaying hammock, yielding himself to the
arms of Morpheus.

With dawn, Mandricardo and Callipygia awoke in
their respective pavilions, and while the Tartar
knight struck the tents and refolded them into

their waterproof casings, the Amazon girl went to investigate Braggadocio's condition.

She found that worthy none the worse for his debauch of yesterday; indeed, he seemed more bright and chipper than she herself felt. He was squatting on a rock, stirring the contents of a tin pan over a small crackling blaze. The delicious odor of scrambling eggs rose to her nostrils as he bade her an affable, "A vurra gude mornin' to ye, moddom, I'm sure! And how's yere ain self this braw new day?"

The eggs, he explained when they had exchanged civilities, came from a nest of duck's eggs he had been keeping his eye on for just such an emergency as this: in Terra Magica, you never quite know when unexpected guests may be dropping in and staying for breakfast, no, not even when you are gallivanting about the world in a Wandering Garden.

"A stout rosher o' bacon would sairtainly perk the meal up the noo, but, losh, me gude moddom, in this life ye canna hae everything!" added Braggadocio. They soon settled down to a piping hot plate of scrambled eggs, which Braggadocio tackled with gusto. Callipygia was hungry enough, but as for Mandricardo, the Tartar was still feeling the ravages of last night's bout with the bottomless black jug, and only picked halfheartedly at his meal.

After breakfast, Mandicardo got out his kit and began oiling and polishing his armor, as a good knight-errant should, plying the lance oil and the buckle polish and whatever, and honing his sword and poignard with a whetstone, applying himself vigorously. Taking the hint, Braggadocio hauled out his dilapidated collection of junk and began scraping off rust and honing and polishing himself, all the while regaling the Tartar with tales and anecdotes of a humorous nature, culled from his immense store of the same, proving himself a raconteur of no mean gifts.

"And then there's the ain aboot . . . whurra, me gude sor, this ain's a mosterpiece . . . 'A knicht oot o' far Cappadocia,' " he began, but just then both became aware of a sinking sensation in the pit of their stomachs. It was not a matter of having taken aboard a few eggs past their prime, no, the sensation was more akin to what you feel when you descend in a high-speed elevator.

"The Garden is coming down—somewhere," remarked the Amazon princess, strolling up. She had busied herself grooming and currycombing their mounts, including poor bony old Rosie, as the man with the walrus mustache called his gauntribbed nag. This last looked not to have had a good grooming for all the weeks she had been imprisoned in the magical flying bower with her master.

The precise location of this "somewhere" was not at once discernible. Quite likely, one island in the tropics looks very much like another, and, as they had come down somewhere in the Seas Below Hind, they were in the tropics.

The Wandering Garden, it seemed, had settled to earth in the boggy and humid interior of the jungle isle of Taprobane, for they were not long in discovering its identity. They were in the midst of a dense forest of mangroves and up to their ankles in muddy swamp water. The air was fetid and steamy; moss hung like tangled gray beards

from branches wherefrom sluggish vipers as thick
as a boy's arm swayed writhing; gaudy orchids
blazed with rich hues. Oh, it was Taprobane, all
right.

It appeared that their unexpected arrival had
disturbed various of the denizens of the man-
grove swamp in the middle of their breakfast, for
a chorus of angry hoots, screeches and bellows
arose in a chorus to greet them as they came to
the edge of the Garden and peered out between
the trees. Among those in view were the doglike
Cephus whose teats give blue milk, and the Tregelaphus which is half deer and half ox. There
were also several quaint and curious Myrmecoles,
whose front halves resemble lions while their hin-
der parts are those of huge red ants.*

Also in residence they found the triple-headed
Senad, to say nothing of a clutch or gaggle of
fearsome Palmipeds. These last monstrosities sob
like children, chuckle like hags, and eat nothing
less excellent than man. A gigantic hybrid like a
huge black stag with a bull's head and seventy-
four white horns which were hollow and through
which the wind either moaned or whistled, de-
pending on the strength of the breeze, could be
glimpsed in the distance, munching on bloated
yellow fungi.

Several large, red-furred day-flying bats were
flapping about through the mist. These were much
larger than was particularly pleasant to behold.

"A disteenctly *on*wholesome dommed feelthy
place!" remarked Sir Braggadocio with a severe,

---

* As if this were enough to make them look odd, the poor
Myrmecoles have reversed genitals. How uncomfortable!

disapproving sniff, taking a hasty swig from his jug to ward off jungle fever.

Hastily clambering into his suit of armor, Mandricardo took the Magic Carpet aloft to reconnoiter their situation predicament. They could not stay here much longer, for Acrasia's Garden was slowly but steadily sinking with a throaty gurgle into the swamp. Fortunately, he spotted a level plain about a league distant with the domes and spires of an exotic foreign city twinkling in the morning sun beyond.

It took four trips to fly all of them out, and their steeds, and the plump, good-natured little mule, Minerva, and their luggage—of the which, Braggadocio had a surprising amount, for besides his cooking and camping gear, his armor, such as it was, and hammock, there were two enormous valises, the lawn chair, which folded up rather neatly, and a clutter of bags and boxes, packages and parcels.

"Hoot, a mon canna ken in advance wha' he'll need on his trovels and odventures in this sorra world," was his philosophical comment on the matter. Which was followed by another libation from the bottomless jug, to shield him against the attack of the dreaded tsetse fly.

Mandricardo had taken everything off the Magic Carpet and was busy strapping his and Callipygia's saddlebags on the withers of Bayardetto, his black charger, and the Amazon girl's Blondel, and loading the rest of Minerva's back, prior to taking off on the Carpet for a more salubrious clime, when Callipygia touched his arm.

"Oh, look," she said, "there are some people from that city over there, riding across the plain to say hello!"

"Dashed nice of them," puffed the Tartar, rolling up the last pile of blankets. "Hospitable, what? May get an invitation to lunch from the blighters . . ."

"A-weel, I dinna think so," said Braggadocio in gloomy tones. "The dommed heathen are riding straight for us, weeth leveled spears."

And so they were, and there were a goodly number of them, too. *Stout lookin' chaps*, thought Ricardo, gnawing on the ends of his droopy moustache. They wore baggy full pantaloons in gay hues—watermelon-pink, pistachio, pastel blue, orange—and Persian slippers with curled-up toes; huge gold hoops bobbled in their earlobes, and their heads (which were shaved bald, except for a pigtail which hung down behind) wore red felt fezzes complete with tassels. They also had thick silk cummerbunds and little red vests, brass armlets and wristlets, and a jangle of bangles about their necks.

More importantly, and to the point, they bore javelins and small round targes like the one Callipygia carried, and each was armed with a huge glittering scimitar. The officers wore enormous fat turbans of richly-colored silk kerchiefs, to which were pinned by aigrets of rubies or emeralds (or, in the case of the second lieutenants, fresh-water pearls) white egret plumes.

Well, anyway, the travelers were led into the capital of Taprobane (whose name they did not happen to catch, the city I mean, nor can I find it recorded in any of the histories at my disposal which record aught of matters Taprobanian), and were granted an audience with the King of the country, whose name they also did not manage to catch, but it was Bunnassa, the son of Busannas, the grandson of Bannussa, and great-grandson of Bussanan. He was a hectic and harried-looking little man, skinny and thin-faced, and with a nervous tic under his left eye. When, just a bit later, they met his mother, they came to understand the reason for the tic.

The King greeted them politely enough, so politely enough that it was difficult for them to figure out if they were actually under arrest or not, and if they were, for *what.* The troops they had encountered there on the grassy plain had been equally equivocal, if you take my meaning. While Mandricardo was all for out-sword and fall-on, and Callipygia also had nothing against a lusty pitched battle, their spirits were somewhat dampened, as far as martial endeavors went, to note the second troop. The first were spearmen who greeted them respectfully enough, requesting them to accept their escort to the capital, for an audience with the king.

The second troop were mounted archers, who remained out of reach of swords, arrows nocked and at the ready. And of the three, only Mandricardo wore full armor.

While King Bunnassa hemmed and hawed, making small talk and obviously stalling for time until the arrival of Someone, the Tartar knight strove to keep calm and to keep his wits about him. They nibbled on sweetmeats and canapes and sampled a few exotic fruits, all the while waiting for ... *whom?*

Then the Dowager Queen Anbussna, the king's mother, sailed into the room as majestically as a galleon under full sail, and they realized for whom they had been waiting: the Power behind the

Throne. The Queen Mother had steel-colored hair, a sharp nose, thin lips pursed in a permanent sniff of disapproval, and an eye that could have been used for splitting logs in the teak forests of Borneo. With her was a large, plump, ecclesiastical-looking personage, who turned out to be the local Bishop and also Pontiff of the Taprobanian National Church.

He gave them the sort of look a man gives to something with several legs which has just crawled out of the salad he had been in the process of eating . . . and Mandricardo got the idea that they were all in a lot of trouble.

4

Heresy in Taprobane

"Are these the culprits, Bunnassa?" inquired the Queen Mother, looking over Mandricardo, Callipygia and Braggadocio with the sort of glare you would give a dog who had just done something on the livingroom carpet you had trained him not to do.

"Yes Mummy, please Mummy," said the king.

"Oh, I say, 'culprits' is a bit harsh, what?" protested the Tartar knight. "I am hight Sir Mandricardo of Tartary, and this lady is hight the Princess Callipygia of Amazonia, and this fella here—"

"Is he *also* hight something?" inquired Queen Anbussna with more than a touch of sarcasm in her tones, which were nasal. She looked Braggadocio up and down, then shuddered all over, which took a bit of time, since there was quite a bit of her to be shuddered.

"Braggadocio, moddom, and a gude morning to ye," said that worthy, with a bow that threatened to precipitate him into her lap. It is more than possible that she got a whiff or two of his breath, as the

wind was blowing in her direction through the
open windows of the throne room: anyway, she
glared at the red-nosed reprobate as though he
were some dreg of society who had just been ap-
prehended in the act of slipping a couple of ounces
of cocaine to some other dreg.

"What, pray tell, is the charge?" demanded
Callipygia. Always of a practical mind, the Amazon girl liked to get past these civilities, if civilities
is quite the word, and down to business.

"Heresy, my poor, misguided young woman,"
said the Bishop, speaking for the first time, and in
the most unctuous and bishoply tones. "To wit,
employing sorcery within the precincts of the realm,
in contradiction of national laws against the practice of same."

"Sorcery? *What* sorcery?"

The Bishop pointed out that the use of Magic
Flying Carpets on Taprobanian soil constituted an
act of sorcery, which was clearly heretical according to the precepts of the Taprobanian national
religion, which was not very unlike that of the
Brachmans of Hindoostan. Using such carpets was,
in short, something unpleasantly close to a miracle.

"And only the accredited saints of the Taprobanian Church are licensed to perform miracles,"
he added in tones of stern reproof.

"Oh, for the love of—!" cried Cally, in exasperated
exasperation. Mandricardo bridled, I think I mean
bridled, and muttered a Tartar expression which
perhaps I should leave untranslated. As for Braggadocio, he remarked something about "dommed
feelthy heathen," and took a brief restorative swig
from his magic jug.

As for the Queen Mother, she drew herself up
and subjected the three of them to a withering

glance, with much the air of a party-giving dowager about to obliterate a trio of gate-crashers.

"Put these persons under restraint," she decreed, looking down her nose at them like a crack shot sighting down a gun barrel.

"Yes, Mummy," said King Bunnassa, and he slunk cringing to the door to tap a gong and summon a clutch of guards.

"Dash it all, some bally days it just doesn't pay to even get up!" complained Mandricardo to his lady-love.

He was right; and this was obviously one of them.

The dungeons in Taprobane, at any rate, were extraordinarily comfortable, of their kind. The floor was covered with Persian carpets, the walls with Frankish tapestries, and the furniture was teakwood, inlaid with mother-of-pearl. There were even brass bowls of fruit standing here and there about on small tabourets.

"Oh, I say! Ker-hem! Visitors!" remarked a small, round, red-faced and very bald man as they were thrust into the room and the door locked and bolted behind them. He wore full armor, all except for his helm, which lay in his lap, half full of walnuts which he as cracking (using the hinged visor for that purpose) and upon the meats of which he was munching.

He politely rose, bowed to Callipygia, peered curiously through his spectacles at Sir Braggadocio—he wore tiny little old fashioned spectacles on wire frames, which rather made him look like portraits of Benjamin Franklin, except that Franklin had more hair—and they all exchanged "hights." I presume that you know by now what that means; if not, then you have merely been skipping through *Kesrick*, *Dragonrouge* and *Mandricardo*. "Hight" is what knights say to each other.

After learning who they were, the fat little old knight drew himself up to his full height of five-foot-four-inches, and bowed again, saying: "Hem! Pleased to meecha, I'm sure. I am hight Sir Murgatroyd Marmaduke Montmorency Mortimer Montgomery de Malaprop," he said in a prissy little voice. "I expect you will have heard of me, ker-*haff*."

"No, can't say that we have," said Mandricardo. De Malaprop fixed him with a glare of reproof.

"Name of de Malaprop, I said, Haff! Seventeen years come Whitsuntide, you know, I've been on the quest of the Galumphing Beast. Ring any bells, young felly—'Galumphing Beast'—?"

"Well, raw'ther!" said Mandricardo, just to be polite. Malaprop looked mollified; in fact, he actually beamed.

"Heff! Yes, dreadful creature! Weary of the chase by now, of course. Still and all, family obligation, what? 'Curse of the de Malaprops' they call it."

"Is it anything like the Blatant Beast that Sir Pelleas was also pursuing, back in the old days?" inquired Callipygia.

"Or the Questing Beast that whatzizname, King Pellinore, was after?" asked Mandricardo. Malaprop positively beamed, turning pink to the tips of his ears.

"Quite like, actually. Your Galumphing Beast is also headed like a serpent, footed like a hare, body of a pard, haunches of your lion, you know, and makes a noise in his tummy like a roomful of

people drinkin' an' laughin' an' tryin' to talk above
very loud music. Only difference is in his gait, you
know: he *galumphs* ... that's sort of half way
between a gallop and a lope. That's why they call
him the Galumphing Beast. Keff! Have a walnut?"

They declined the offer. From behind his helmet he abstracted a cigar, the which he lit and
puffed upon, after politely begging permission
from Callipygia.

He listened while Mandricardo explained they
had been slammed in prison on charges of heresy.
"Hell's bones," remarked the fat little knight in
conversational tones, "but so am I. For being a
blankety-blanked foreigner, by golly, blank me in
the blank-blank!" Then, noticing Callipygia again,
the bald little knight pinked all over the parts of
him visible, and said, "Beg poddon, I'm sure. Par'm
my Chaldean, ma'm!"

Cally grinned and assured the little man he was
par'med. She had conceived a sudden fondness
for the fat little man. So, for that matter, had
Braggadocio, who proffered his black jug. Obviously one to take a chance, Sir Malaprop (he asked
them to call him that, for short), took a hefty swig,
pinked, gargled a bit, swallowed manfully, then
took a deep breath.

"Very smooth, ker-haff! Er, haw! *Quite* smooth,
dammy. And if you don't mind, I'll just have another drittle link ... hem! I mean, a drother nittle
link. Kaff!" Without further words, he upended
the black jug and gurgled for a time. When he
lowered it, he was *quite* a bit pinker, but seemed
none the worse for the experience.

"Most stronery beverage," he remarked, resum-
ing his normal coloration.

"Most extraordinary, indeed," admitted Mandricardo. "Have you been here long?"

"Long enough," admitted Sir Malaprop, giving the end of his cigar a glare of reproof.* "Flew here on a bally winged horse, you know. While pursuin' the Beast. Got slapped in gaol on charges of heresy, sorcery, dammy knows what! Bally place, this! Pass the jug."

For a time they discussed ways and means of exiting from the present predicament. Sir Malaprop was disinclined to believe that they could expect mercy from what Sir Braggadocio called "the dommed feelthy heathen."

"What I mean is, the Taprobanians, eh? Can you expect the leopard to change his socks, what?" he said in his prissy tones—and Mandricardo began to realize how the fat, bald, red-faced little knight had earned his sobriquet of "Malaprop." For it was either a sobriquet or a surname, and if a sobriquet, then it was one that was certainly singularly appropriate.

He paused once again to refresh himself from Braggadocio's bottomless jug. Lowering it at length, he coughed phlegmily for a time, wiped watering eyes, remarked, "S-smooth!", puffed again on his cigar, and returned the jug to its owner. Braggadocio took a swig or twelve himself, and explained how it, the jug, that is, had been a gift from a grateful sorcerer.

"Should have a statute directed to him, ker-humph!" said the little knight. Unexpectedly, Callipygia giggled like a schoolgirl.

"You mean . . . he should have a statue *erected* to him," she said. The red-faced knight gave her a frosty glare.

---

* It had gone out while he was *glug-glugging*.

"Thought that was what I said, ma'm," he snapped. Braggadocio passed him the jug.

Mandricardo had been roaming about, during this exchange of conversation, examining the walls and the windows. These were few, and small, and heavily barred.

"I say," he muttered, "any chances of escaping from here, what?" Sir Malaprop correctly assumed the query was directed at himself. He lowered Braggadocio's jug, and pursed his lips judiciously.

"Hem! Kaff! Excellent thought! We must explore every stone and leave no avenue unturned, as the felly said. Karf!"

Callipygia turned pink and began to giggle again, turning away from Malaprop's glare of reproof. She had just fallen helplessly in love with the fat little knight—not, of course, the sort of love she felt for Mandricardo, but something of the emotion you feel for an appealing puppy who keeps falling on its face and making a mess on the carpet—and every misspoken word that fell from his lips was a priceless gem to her. You will have to forgive Callipygia for this, I'm afraid.

They passed a lazy afternoon, what with Braggadocio's jug and all.

Later on, Mandricardo noticed from one of the barred windows the Queen Mother strolling in the palace gardens, accompanied by two bouncing girls. They were fully grown (even a bit past their prime), but bounced and cavorted like small children.

"Oh, them; yes, of course," said Malaprop, when the Tartar inquired of them. "His Majesty's sisters, you know. Princess, let me see, now, yes, Princess Assbunna, and the other one is Princess Abnussna. Not that anybody ever calls them by

their real names, of course. It's 'Lucie' and 'Goosie'
and don't ask *me* why. Nice gels, I guess . . . well
behaved."

"They certainly obey the Queen," remarked
Callipygia, for the Queen Mother had just snapped
a brief word to the two, who were swinging back
and forth on the garden gate, and they came
scampering obediently at her heels.

"Yes, ker-kaph! The velvet hand in the iron
glove, as the felly says . . ." muttered Sir Malaprop, and then wondered why the Amazon had
gone all pink and giggly. Could it have been something that he had said?

Once a day, it seemed, the prisoners were to be
permitted a stroll through the gardens, if for purely
humanitarian reasons. Sunshine and fresh air, and
all that sort of thing. Under heavy guard, of course,
which was only to be expected. On their first such
stroll, they encountered the Queen Mother. Kneel-
ing on a velvet cushion, she was at her gardening,
hacking about in the flower beds with a small but
destructive fork. The Queen was a gardener of
the ruthless type, and went for any small green
thing that incautiously showed a timid small spike
above the surface of the soil, suspecting it of being
a Weed.

They bade her a polite good afternoon, to which
she replied glacially. It was as if the North Pole
had spoken, and she bent upon them the sort of
Look that could pry open a clam at thirty feet.

Just then, Lucie and Goosie came bounding up,
hand in hand. Lucie and Goosie never seemed to
walk like other people: they skipped and gamboled,
scampered and frisked, as if to demonstrate how
very girlish an age was thirty-four and thirty-five.
Looking as if it pained her to have to do it, the

Queen Mother introduced the new prisoners to the girls, who twisted the ends of their pigtails, giggled, eyed the stalwart Tartar shyly, then raced off to jump over the hedges and frolic about.

After their brisk stroll about the gardens, they were herded back to durance vile. Callipygia remarked on the Queen Mother's frigid manner: with a little smile, she said, "I'm afraid that woman has taken a strong dislike to us. I fear we shall never get her to change her mind and like us, so there's not much point even in being polite."

"Ga-humph!" coughed Sir Malaprop, to show agreement with her views in the manner. Then he added, as he so often did, that one cannot expect the leopard to change his socks . . . and there was that bally Amazon girl, blushing and giggling again.

"Ker-*hapf!*" he said severely, bending upon the offending young woman a glare of frosty reproof.

Callipygia only went off into further muffled giggles. How stronery! thought Sir Malaprop. Could it have been anything he said?

. . . Surely not!

5

The Bronze Ring, Again

They were served a perfectly adequate dinner which consisted of six courses, plus soup, and their choice of red or white wine. The national cuisine of Taprobane, they discovered, leaned rather heavily toward breadfruit, coconuts, paw-paws, mangoes, bananas, and a wide variety of sea-food. Mandricardo munched gamely away, but would dearly have cherished a good saddle of mutton or prime ribs of beef.

Anyway, it would seem that the Taprobanians, whatever else they had in mind for the latest batch of heretics and sorcerers to fall into their clutches, had no intentions of trying to starve them to death. But, since the penalty for heresy and for sorcery, under Taprobanian law, was death, Mandricardo could not help wondering, a little uneasily, why the Taprobanians were taking so long to get around to it.

Not that he was in any particular hurry to be executed, you will understand, but a man does like to have things done neatly and with dispatch.

Sir Malaprop, munching noisily on a mango, came up with the most likely answer, which was only to be expected, since he had been here many weeks longer than the rest of them, ever since his winged horse had unexpectedly thrown him, which was how he had gotten captured in the first place,* and he was thus their resident expert on Matters Taprobanian.

"Hem! Waitin' for the most favorable planetary conjunction, I expect," was his explanation for the curious delay. "These bally heathen are bugged on h'astrology, the narsty lot of 'em. Nearly as bad as A-rabs. Hemff! Beggin' yer par'm, I'm sure," he added, with an apologetic glance at Mandricardo. For some reason, he seemed to think that the Tartar knight was an Arab. There is no explaining these things. Tartars are not Arabs, nor are Arabs Tartars, but, then, when you have spent the last seventeen years of your life chasing after a Galumphing Beast, you are entitled to get a little pixilated.

"Not at all," said Mandricardo, moodily, in response to the begging-of-his-pardon. "Wonder when the next favorable conjunction will be, what?"

"Tomorrow mornin'," said Sir Malaprop, relighting his cigar.

As you might very well expect, *that* news jolted them just a little. Sir Braggadocio had made the mistake of having just taken a mouthful of *usquebae*, which he swallowed the wrong way and had to be slapped on the back by Callipygia, and then thumped between the shoulders by Sir Mandri-

---

* Come to think of it, he never did get around to explaining about the winged horse, how he had found it and all. Pity. But then your true knight never brags about his deeds and exploits.

cardo, when he continued to gag and choke and cough.

"Gadzooks," said Mandricardo feebly. "Tomorrow, you say, what?"

"Tomorrow *mornin'*," Malaprop corrected him. Mandricardo paled, as much as a Tartar, with his swarthy skin, *can* pale, and swallowed the lump in his throat. He reached out and took a swig from the bottomless black jug which Braggadocio, wordlessly, passed to him.

"Wonder if the bally Beast will miss me," said Malaprop in rather melancholy tones. "Father to son, father to son, h'it's been many a year—generations—since the first Malaprop pursued the Galumphing Beast, you know." He swallowed a lump in his own throat which was, I am sure, no smaller than the one which Mandricardo had just circumvented.

"Blanked Beast won't know what's happening in the world, or what the world's coming to, without a de Malaprop pursuin' him, what? Ker-*huff!*"

He subsided, looking glum and gloomy.

"Pass the jug, dammy!" he added.

Callipygia had paled too, but set her small determined jaw firmly. She had her arms crossed upon her breast and with one hand was restlessly twisting and turning the bronze ring with the strange runes upon it which she had worn on her biceps since finding the ring, or armlet, in the Troll's cave.

"I just wish we had the Carpet—*then* we could get out of here," she said absently.

In the next split second the wall exploded into flying bricks and chunks of mortar, plaster and wood. They took hasty refuge under the table and Malaprop rolled under the sofa. However, nothing further occurred. Peering cautiously out they discovered the Magic Flying Carpet hovering about eleven inches off the floor and quivering with energy. It was covered with brick dust and bits of plaster, but seemed otherwise unharmed.

"Well, kem! I will be double blank-blanked in the blankety-blank *blank!*" said Sir Malaprop in the ringing silence. Then, realizing himself, the ends of the tips of his ears glowed pinkly and he said, "Haff! Kakk! Par'm my Sanskrit, ma'm!"

"You're par'med," said Cally.

Your historian does not exactly know how to explain to his readers precisely how and why so bright a girl as Callipygia, to say nothing of Mandricardo, *et al*, commonly have failed thus far in this true and veracious History to have figured out that when Callipygia makes a wish, and twists on that bronze Trollish ring she wears on her biceps, and the wish promptly comes true, why, I say, they can't realize that the ring is a *Magic Wishing Ring*.

In real life, of course, you or I or any of us would guess it the truth after Wish Number One. But, so far since the Amazon princess found the ring in the Troll's cave and put it on, she had wished Mandricardo to Aegypt, herself a thousand miles across a chasm, the Flying Carpet through the dungeon wall, and I don't know how much else. But somehow or other, and bright as she was, without question, Cally had thus far failed to add two to two and come up with four.

I merely report these facts, I don't invent them, you know. Take a good look at the *Chronicle Narrative of the Deeds of Mandricardo* if you don't believe me. . . .

*   *   *

The four of them blinked rather dazedly at the
hole which the irresistible force of the Magic Flying
Carpet had just punched through the seemingly-
solid masonry of their dungeon wall (which, like
most dungeon walls, was strongly and stoutly con-
structed, for rather obvious reasons), and whose
irresistible force was, I have no doubt, nor did my
characters, aided (when they finally figured the
thing out) by the equally irresistible force of
Callipygia's wishing ring.

And the prisoners wasted no time at all in climbing aboard; in fact, Cally was the only one to
loiter, piling loose bricks into a heap on the Carpet, which hung about two feet above the floor,
throbbing and vibrating restlessly.

"Why the bricks?" inquired Sir Malaprop inter-
estedly, as he snatched up his box of cigars, emp-
tied the ripe walnuts out of his helm, and clambered
aboard the Carpet.

"They may come in handy,' " said Cally grimly,
"in case we have opposition. We are none of us
armed, remember."

"Ker-hem!" said Sir Malaprop lamely. "Well,
dammy, where to, then?"

"First of all, the stables," declared Mandricardo.
"Dashed if I'll leave Bayardetto behind!"

"Or me, Blondel," said Callipygia. "Or, for that
matter, dear little Minerva."

"My winged horse will have flown on by this
time," said Sir Malaprop sadly. "However, I agree
with your sentiments! And the demmed creature
was not the most comfortable steed to ride, to be
perfectly prank, I mean, prepctly fank—"

"We know what you mean," said Callipygia. The
Carpet, with all of them aboard, zoomed out

through the hole it had made in the wall on its
way in, and they zipped across the gardens, clip-
ping the tops of the taller hedges. Lucie and Goosie,
frolicking on the greensward, yipped and fell on
their noses. So did four and twenty guardsmen,
trotting under full arms to investigate the reported
breaking-and-entering, or jailbreak, or whatever
you want to call it. They dropped so fast their
fezzes went rolling and their scimitars got tangled
up. The one or two who were far enough away as
to be beyond Carpet-reach, leveled bows and things
but a few well-thrown bricks put an end to *that*.

In the dungeon stables they found Bayardetto
and Blondel and Minerva and Braggy's bony nag
placidly munching cornmeal and bran. The
steeds eyed them with mild interest, but, as the
Taprobanians filled an excellent trough, went right
on eating while their masters and mistress lugged
their saddles on them and strapped them into
place. While Mandricardo and the Amazon girl
were attending to this, Braggadocio and Sir Malaprop found the missing luggage piled in a dry
corner and promptly loaded it upon the Carpet,
which obligingly stretched itself out by some method
known only to Magic Carpets, so as to accommodate all of them, plus the fat little newcomer,
whose winged horse had, as he himself had predicted, flown on.*

Braggadocio, brandishing his dented, nicked and
still rusty claymore, peered out the stable door,

---

* If it wasn't Pegasus (and surely Sir Malaprop would have mentioned it by name if it had been the famous Pegasus), then possibly it was Crysaor, Pegasus' very-overlooked and little-known twin.
I would say twin-*brother*, but actually, I'm none too certain as to
the gender of Crysaor. For that matter, come to think of it, I'm
not sure of the gender of Pegasus, either.

and took a brief restorative swig from his jug to fortify himself against the coming conflict.

"Sae far, sae gude," he remarked grimly. "But yon feelthy heathen'll be oop to their dommed tricks, weel do I ken it—"

"Ker-*humph!* They certainly are," said Malaprop. "And here they come, this time with elephants—"

"Hoot, mon! Gude losh, do ye ken nowt better than to worra aboot a dommed gert elephant more or less, when we hae a Mogic Carpet at our ain deesposal?" And he hopped upon the vibrile piece of floor-covering, which had now stretched itself out to the proportions of an Olympic swimming-pool in order to accommodate Mandricardo, Callipygia, Braggadocio and Malaprop, as well as their beasts and all their luggage.

They flew straight at the row of elephants (there were four of them, and war-elephants at that, with wooden castles on their backs, loaded to the scuppers with bowmen, and each elephant also brandished a great war-axe in the loop of its trunk, as big as a battering ram and thrice as heavy.

However, at their first astonished glimpse at the amazing flying thing whizzing straight for them, and bristling with men and woman and horses and mule and lots of luggage, and fluttering *with a vengeance*, the war-elephants flinched, and headed for the hills, the mahouts leaping off into the bushes or whatever, and in no time worth talking about, the encounter was over.

Knights one, Taprobanians nothing, was the final score.

BOOK TWO

The Ogre's Den

6

Carpet to the Rescue!

Well, in virtually no time at all, they had soared over the domes and roofs, between the spires and minarets and whatnot, and were beyond the walls of the Taprobanian capitol and zooming along at a good clip across the grassy plain.

The Carpet, for Carpetly reasons of its own, no doubt, seemed to be keeping a low profile, in the truest and original sense of that term. That is to say, it was flying rather close to the ground ... rather uncomfortably close, and well within arrow-shot or spear-cast. Neither was it by this time flying all that fast, either—at least, not as fast as it had from time to time on previous occasions.

The reasons for this are not all that obvious, and, as the *Chronicle Narrative* notes the fact but does not attempt to give its readers any explanation thereof, I will take a chance and hazard a guess of my own—to wit, that it had probably been quite a very long time in its checkered past history, since the Magic Flying Carpet had been called upon by its master to sustain and transport

so unusually heavy a burden as one Tartar knight
in full armor, with charger; one pleasingly-plump
Amazon princess, with roan mare; one walrus-
mustached Caledonian prevaricator, complete with
bony old nag and an amazing lot of luggage and
one stout, red-faced little knight like Sir Malaprop. To say nothing of the luggage loaded on
the little mule, Minerva, which included the still
heavy picnic lunch basket from Amazonia and the
folded-up palanquins which belonged to Mandricardo and Callipygia, together with all their own
luggage.

No wonder the Carpet was not quite as perky as
usual!

"They are following us," said Callipygia. They
looked over their shoulders and saw that she had
correctly reported the conditions to their rear.
Not by the war-elephants, of course. Those had all
run away to the hills, sagacious beasts that they
are. (Your war-elephant knows when to fold his
tent and call it a day, and when your foe starts
bringing out his Flying Carpets, you call it a day.)

No, there were no elephants, but quite a lot of
angry-looking spearmen and an even larger number of even angrier-looking horse-archers, and in
front of them all rode the Bishop, puffing and
purple in the face, and bouncing up and down in
the saddle. This pontiff seemed determined to see
to it that such heretics and sorcerers should not
escape the righteous vengeance of the Taprobanian
National Church.

"Hmm," said Sir Mandricardo to himself. Not at
all a devious man, but one given to resolving all
problems by the sword (or whatever weapon lay
closest to hand), he was not inclined to just run
away from the Bishop of Taprobane, but to somehow do him in.

They were, in their flight, approaching the outskirts (or whatever you want to call them) of the swampy area in which they had first landed here in the Wandering Garden. They remembered it as having been rather boggy and sad, and with a lot of fat vipers, and lianas, and moldering trees behung and bedangle with Spanish moss, whatever that is, and suchlike. *Just* the very place for pursuing horsemen to get bogged in and sucked down and so on.

Sir Mandricardo directed the Magic Carpet to fly directly out over the swamp, toward its center. Now, I will have to admit at this point that neither the *Chronicle Narrative* nor any other of the texts I have consulted give me the slightest notion of exactly how you *direct* the Magic Flying Carpet. Outside of the simple fact that you say, "Fly, Carpet!" to get it started, I don't know the further details. The *Chronicle Narrative* doesn't say,* and I just plain don't know. And, since this is a true and veracious history, well, I wouldn't *dare* make it up, now would I?

"They're following us into the swamp," said Callipygia.

"Yon braying jockoss of a Beeshop weel soon be regretting it, the noo," crowed Sir Braggadocio, hefting his dented claymore and fortifying the inner man with another swig from his bottomless black jug. Wiping, and then, thoughtfully, gnawing on his mustache, he broke into some keening song or other in what we have to suppose to have been Gaelic, since no one present could under-

* Neither do any of the *Thief of Baghdad* movies, in their various incarnations, nor the story of Housain in the *Arabian Nights*, nor any other source available to me. Sorry.

stand a word of it. After a chorus or two, he rolled over and fell asleep, the magic jug pillowed against his armored chest. As far as Sir Braggadocio was concerned, "the whole sorra business" was concluded.

"Oh, my goodness, dammy!" huffed Sir Malaprop. They had not found his luggage, nor his sword, and he kept clasping one fat little fist futilely at his waist, where the prized blade would ordinarily have hung. Callipygia, who sensed the brave and knightly spirit within the bald and pudgy little man—for it is truly and forever *the inner man* who counts, and the outward show is so much meaningless persiflage, as all of us must know, by now, friends—Callipygia sorrowed for him and mightily wished that he had his old, accustomed blade hanging at his hip.

Unfortunately, she was not clutching and twisting that queer old bronze Troll's ring on her upper arm when she wished. But that is the way the world wags. . . .

The Bishop (and Pontiff) of the Taprobanian National Church, who was leading the chase, anxious, as you might well understand, not to let a clutch of heretics and sorcerers elude the Execution Block and the Headsman, was riding hot on their heels. So to speak, that is, since one thing a Magic Flying Carpet does *not* have is heels.

When they plunged into, or slightly over, the swamp, so did he, and never mind the mud that splashed to his hips and the wriggling vipers that flew by, and all those monsters we have already mentioned. And as he, their leader, plunged into the swamp, well, quite naturally, so did all those spearmen and archers and whatever. (I really cannot be held accountable for these military terms, being a civilian born and bred, myself.)

Skimming the treetops, the heavily-laden Carpet flew into the very midst of the swamp.

The Bishop gamely splashing along at their fore, the troops of Taprobane followed hard on the fringes of the flapping, flying thing.

Quite suddenly—and, also, quite unexpectedly—Mandricardo spotted dead ahead of them, looming through the miasmic mists and vapors, the unmistakable vegetative-mix of the Wandering Garden, still wallowing amidst the fetid waters of the muddy mangroves. Why it had not long ago flown on its unpredictable way, of course, none of them could say; Wandering Gardens are moved by their own mysterious motives, and who am I, a mere author, a teller-of-tales, to understand a Garden?

They flew directly over it, just skimming the tops of the tallest trees. They were chestnut, and olive, and acacia, a palm or two, not to mention a kingly oak, an evergreen, and a quince tree grown quite beyond its accustomed height. But what the hey.

As they soared over the half-submerged Garden, the grim-faced Bishop rode into it from the ground-level, or swamp-level.

He very soon regretted this.

As they, on the huge Carpet, soared off into the east, dwindling at length from view, as they left the happy Isle of Taprobane behind them, the Bishop and his hand-picked men, found themselves, and quite unaccountably, unable to *continue* riding through the Garden.

That is to say, they found it impossible to ride *out* the other side. An invisible and impalpable, but quite unbreakable, barrier resisted them, as Braggadocio himself had earlier discovered.

How they cursed and fussed and fumed, well, I will leave it up to the fertile imagination of my reader to imagine for him or herself, for I cannot say.

Some time after the Carpet, and all aboard, had dwindled into a mere mote in the distance, flying toward the mountainy bulk of Asia, the Wandering Garden, gathering its mysterious resources, rose suckingly up out of the muddy grip of the swamp, and floated away from Taprobane, Bishop and picked troop, and all.

It seemed to be heading in the direction of the Far Antipodes, when last seen. At any rate, the Bishop was never more seen or heard from in the Isle of Taprobane, nor, for that matter, in any of the Isles of India or China. And I not only do not know exactly what became of him, the punctilious rogue, but I do not really care.

I strongly doubt if anybody in Taprobane particularly regretted his passing from amongst their number, with the possible exception of Queen Anbussna.

As for the Magic Flying Carpet, it had reached by then the mainland of Asia, and all aboard were free from Taprobane and its laws.

And, as the feller says, "out of the frying pan and into the fire." But the proof of that will shortly be demonstrated.

It was sundown by now, but while there was still enough light to see by, Sir Mandricardo steered, if that's the word I really want, steered a course north and east from Taprobane, which would in time take them back to the mainland of Asia. In the meantime, they had quite a lot of ocean to traverse, and the Magic Carpet was so heavily laden that it skimmed the waves as it hurtled on its way to land.

The humans and their steeds and luggage had huddled together toward the middle of the Carpet, perhaps because of the illusion that there is some safety in numbers. The cold evening wind, stinging with salt spray, whipped in their faces, and the sun went down somewhere behind Taprobane in a welter of gold and crimson gore.

They had little or nothing to say between them; the ebullition of escape had left them by now, and they felt empty and listless and rather weary. Excitement always leaves a sour aftertaste in your mouth, once it is over and your heart had has ceased pumping adrenalin through your veins.

It got a lot colder, and the spray a lot wetter. Braggadocio passed his magic bottomless black jug around and they all took a fortifying swig therefrom, even Callipygia. She purpled, grimaced, strangled a little, and thought the bitter and smoky stuff tasted of lance oil and buckle polish . . . but it *did* warm your tummy.

None of them could remember what land lay next to Hindoostan on the coast, not that it mattered very much. Whatever land it was, they would be visiting it rather soon.

Flying fish cut the black waters about them as they flew. The Moon came up over the edge of the world and flooded the land and the sea with her cold glory. They got chillier, and also hungry and sleepy. After a time, Callipygia curled up next to Mandricardo and slept. He untied his lion-skins and draped them over her to help keep her warm. Braggadocio and Malaprop, passing the jug back and forth, sang a few drowsy verses of "*Scots wha hae,*" and began to snore. Eventually, even Mandricardo nodded.

None of them was awake enough to know it
when at length, and after some hours, the Carpet
settled gently to earth.

Dawn found them wide awake and jubilant. To
have escaped from the Isle of Taprobane was
enough to put them all in a good mood, especially
Sir Malaprop who had languished, if that is quite
the word, for some weeks in the rather luxurious
Taprobanian equivalent of a gaol.

Callipygia was up before dawn, ranging the
marshes with her bow, hoping to bring down a
brace of plump sea-fowl. She had no luck in her
search, but she did find a dozen or thirteen eggs
in various nests amidst the reeds, which she brought
back to their camp and they cooked them in Braggadocio's skillet, seasoning the scrambled eggs with
the last of the smoked oysters and paté from the
huge picnic lunch the Queen of the Amazons had
packed for them.

Breakfast was scrumptious, with plenty of hot
black tea and a dab of caviar for each of them.

Mandricardo did not dare use the Carpet. It
was old and worn, dusty and threadbare, and had
developed a tear or two, which he could not mend,
lacking needle and thread. They would have to
ride horseback from here on, all except for poor
Sir Malaprop, that is, whose flying horse had flown
off somewhere during his captivity in Taprobane.
No matter, they decided: they would load the
luggage aboard the Carpet, command it to float
along behind them, and Malaprop could ride on
Minerva's back. The mule seemed to like carrying
the fat, bald little knight more than luggage,
anyway.

As they rode, they discussed where they were

going. Mandricardo explained, sensibly enough, that he and his fiancée were riding home to Tartary in order to get married and to settle down. He had had about enough of knight-errantry, had Mandricardo, and that went for Callipygia, too.

As for Sir Malaprop, as he explained yet once again, and with many a ker-hem! and hugg-ger*haff!*, that, since, after all, he was merely wandering the world in quest of the Galumphing Beast,* as he had been doing for the last bally seventeen years come next Whitsuntide, hem!, and, whereas the bally Beast could very easily be anywhere at all on the terraquaeus Globe, if *Globe* is quite the word he wanted for a world which happened to be flat as a pancake, then he was perfectly happy* to accompany them on their journey to Tartary.

Callipygia was delighted.

* The Burden and Curse of the de Malaprops, alas!

*What he actually said, was "herfectly pappy," but never mind. Once a de Malaprop, always a de Malaprop, I suppose.

7

The Absconding-With of
Braggadocio

While it was a matter of some indifference to Sir
Malaprop where his travels took him, since the
Galumphing Beast could as easily be in one part
of the world of Terra Magica as in another, things
were somewhat different with Braggadocio. He
was a bit more selective.

Since leaving Fairyland, he informed them, he
had been trying to find his way back home to
Caledonia, which lay to the north of Albion. And
that country, you will understand, lay in exactly
the opposite direction they were presently traveling. And doubtless he would have been in Caledonia by this time, had it not been for his seeking
refuge for the night in the Wandering Garden of
the Enchantress Acrasia.

"So, me gude sor and moddom, I'll be bidding
ye me fareweels, and, weel, it's customarra in soch
ceercumstonces that feerst we'll drink a wee drap,
but dinna fash yersel', for the twa o' ye—oh,
WHURRA!"

This last was said in a shout; and it is quite

possible, that, had it not been for the Interruption
that happened at that moment, Sir Braggadocio,
who had taken aboard a goodish supply of *usquebae*
thus far in the morning, well, he could easily have
carried on his meandering monologue in this fashion for another half a page or so—had it not been,
I say, for the Interruption.

The Interruption bent down from the top of a
nearby hill and plucked Braggadocio out of the
saddle as easily as you or I would pluck an apple
from the bough. Easier, in fact, since it had hands
the size of livingroom chairs.

Braggadocio kicked and squalled as he was lifted
into the air. His bony nag, Rosie, promptly did the
only sensible thing for a horse to do under the
circumstances, and bolted. So did Blondel and
Bayardetto, and in different directions, too.

As for Minerva, she set her feet carefully and
lowered her head with a dangerous glint in her
eye, showing her teeth just a little above the curl
in her lip. If any Giant or Troll or Ogre was going
to mess with Minerva, he was going to Get Bitten.

Yelling angrily, Sir Mandricardo vanished in a
westerly direction, hidden by a cloud of dust, as
Bayardetto bolted in panicky flight from Whatever-
it-was that had picked up Braggadocio. Callipygia
dug her spurs into Blondel's flanks and drew back
sharply on the reins. Her roan mare whinnied
fearfully, eyeballs rolling, and came to a reluctant
halt. The Amazon girl snatched up targe and spear
and ran to Braggadocio's aid.

The thing that held him fifteen feet in the air,
blinking at him with small, weak eyes—*four* of
them, you would have noticed right off—was too
small to be a Giant (although it sounds sort of silly

to use the word "small" in reference to something as wide as a house and as tall as three or four grown men standing on each other's shoulders. Which meant that he—*it*—was either an Ogre or a Troll, Cally decided, as she hefted the spear.

Braggadocio was kicking and yelling, and, say what you will about the red-nosed man with the walrus mustache, he was certainly no coward. Most men, knights, even, might very well tend to curl up and whimper just a bit, when snatched out of their saddles by Ogres (or by Trolls), but not Braggy.

He was swinging his dented, rusty claymore and roaring as he squirmed and wriggled in the grip of that immense hand: "Whush, ye gert oogly varmint, leave me go the noo, or I'll dommed weel slosh off yere dommed oogly gert nose!"

The Ogre* reached up, pinched the rusty claymore between one enormous thumb and an equally enormous forefinger, wriggled it out of Braggadocio's grasp, and let it fall to the ground, where Malaprop soon retrieved it. Then, dropping the kicking, thrashing knight into the huge sack that hung over his shoulder, and squinting around with tiny weak eyes blinking feebly, through the whirling dust, unable to see any of the others of the party, most of whom were galloping off in all directions, he turned about and waddled away toward his Den. Ogres live in Dens, you know, just like Trolls live in caves. A fantasy writer has to know these things. . . .

The Ogre Grumblegore had left his Den quite

---

* And it had to be an Ogre, because they live in the south while Trolls live in the north. See the Notes to this chapter for my reasons for saying so. I don't just make this stuff *up*, you know.

early that morning because, except for the one
knight in the cage, his larder was very empty, and
an Ogre likes to have victuals in store, since when
you are as big as a house, you generally tend to
have an appetite to match.

Little 'Uns (as Ogres and Giants and such think
of we ordinary mortals) scamper and squeak and
scurry so swiftly that they, the great, slow-footed,
stumbling creatures, often have trouble catching
them. I mean *us*. I suppose that this insures the
survival of our species, at least in Terra Magica,
but it *does* make things a little rough on Ogres,
who have as much of a right to eat dinner as we
do, except perhaps when the dinner they are about
to eat is *us*.

Grumblegore was not particularly annoyed that
he had only caught one of the Little 'Uns, for
together with the one he had already in his cage,
this new one would do just excellently to Sweeten
the Pot. Besides, he had several wagonloads of
Irish potatoes, Spanish onions, cabbages, turnips,
carrots and beets to throw in—

Why, he had enough fixin's to make slumgullion, his favorite stew!

"*Um!*" said Grumblegore, happily, as he waddled along. "Slumgullion's berrer'n *ennythin'!*" And
it was, too: especially when "sweetened" with a
couple of Little 'Uns.

When he got home he upended his sack and
dumped his prize out on his kitchen table. Braggadocio straightened himself out, combed a peck
or two of chicken feathers from his person, preened
his mustache and looked with narrowed eyes at
the monstrous visage—actually, *visages*—which
peered down at him.

His heart sank into his boots, and only rose

again after a restorative swig or two from the bottomless black jug which, "thonk losh!" he had carried on his person when attacked.

There were some several tons of prime Ogre looking him over, and Braggadocio, who was only human, blenched, and looked back. The creature that had captured him was of a degree of ugliness that, heretofore, Braggadocio had only envisioned on those times when the *usquebae* gave him delirium tremens.

"Oh, gude losh, Braggy," he muttered to himself, "ye're in a turrible spot, ye ken, but the whole sorra business 'll be over soon, ye puir fule! Ain gert goolp, and ye're dune fer . . ."

The Ogre, for his part, stared back with a certain culinary interest. It was a knight, then, since it wore bits and pieces of rusted armor; and they were always a trial, prying them out of the can, so to speak.

" 'T's inna can," complained the head on the right-hand side. This head, as Braggadocio soon learned, called itself Dexter; it was the size of a cement mixer and about as pretty as one, thatched with dirty red hair so coarse each strand was as thick as a roofing nail. It had warts the size of pineapples on its huge nose.

"Wull, leastwise hit's summing fer the pot," said the other head, which called itself Lefty.

"Oh, gude losh," said Sir Braggadocio faintly, "the dommed oogly brute talks to it*seelf* . . ." and he sat back on something (it was the saucer which held the Ogre's teacup, as soon shall be seen) and upended the bottomless jug, which *glug-glug-glugged* for a time while the gallant Caledonian restored his bodily fluids.

For the Ogre, you see, had two heads. Not a sight a man wants to see when he is *fully sober*.*

Unable to so much as take a poke at Grumblegore's ankles (thick around as fifty-year-old oak trees, they were) with her spear, Callipygia went in search of the rest of their party. She found Minerva without any trouble, of course, since the staunch little mule had not budged from her spot, and there was Malaprop over there behind some boulders, hemming nervously and cleaning his glasses on a silk handkerchief. But it took quite some time to locate Mandricardo, for his black stallion had gone galloping off, or "pricking across the verdant plain," as Sir Thomas Malory would say, and it took the Tartar knight some little time to quiet down his charger and lead it back toward the scene where they had encountered the Ogre.

They were all pretty well agreed, by this time, that it was an Ogre who had carried off the missing member of their party.

"We've got to go after him," said Callipygia urgently, gesturing toward the hills in the distance with her javelin. "The Ogre went that way."

"Oh, we'll catch the blighter, never fear!" chortled Sir Mandricardo. The Tartar knight was in fine fettle. With nothing against which to pit his knightly prowess in some time, not counting a few fat Taprobanians and a bunch of war-elephants—no *foeman worthy of his steel*, you might say—the Tartar knight looked forward with zest, gusto and considerable enthusiasm to actually crossing swords,

---

* Since it is usually Trolls who have two heads, or more, there is a distinct possibility that our Ogre had some Trollish blood in him. Or do I mean "them?"

or whatever, with a genuine Ogre. It would be a First for him.

Any knight-errant worth his salt would have felt the same way, of course. This was exactly the sort of thing your true knights-errant went around the world *doing*.

Mounting up, they rode toward the foothills, with Sir Malaprop jouncing along astride Minerva's fat rump.

After quite some time, an hour or two at least, they spied the Ogre's castle—or "Den," as they are most properly termed—atop a medium-smallish Alp, or whatever, in the distance. It had to be the Ogre's castle, because ordinary castles don't come as big as this one did . . . but, when you are as tall as three or four fully-grown men standing on each other's shoulders, I suppose you need large rooms to move around in.

Reaching the foot of the mountain, they dismounted and unsaddled their steeds, permitting them to graze the meadow grass, which was rather sparse here in the hills, but any grass is better than none, if you are a horse, and a hungry one. That also goes for mules, too.

"One of us must reconnoiter, what? *I'll* go," said Mandricardo. "You stay here and guard the animals. There may be other Ogres about—"

"*I'll* go; *you* guard the animals," said Callipygia.

"Oh, I say! Dash it all . . ."

"You had the last exploit. Now it's *my* turn," the Amazon girl said firmly.

"What exploit was that?" demanded the Tartar. "You don't mean the Monoceros—?"

"*After* the Monoceros," replied Callipygia. "Long after the Monoceros. Never mind: I've got dibs on this exploit."

Sir Malaprop had just opened his mouth to volunteer to accompany her, even though he was a little too fat around the middle to be much of any good at mountain climbing, but—just then—

A long, wriggling shape, about the size of a young brontosaurus went rapidly over the hill-line. It moved with an odd gait, part gallop and part lope and quite a bit of the peculiar humping way a ferret or a weasel perambulates. It paused directly above, craning its long, long neck to stare down at them with immense, luminous, goggling eyes.

Then it made an interrogative, rather plaintive cry that sounded like sixty people all talking above the juke box in a noisy singles' bar.

And Sir Malaprop got very excited.

"Oh, hell's bones! The Beast! The dear, dear Beast! Not a sign of him in two years, not even a stale fewmet! Where's me lance? *Where's me bally lance?*"

Cally handed him her own lance. His helmet fell off with a resounding clang. He bent over to pick up his helmet and dropped the lance. Eventually, they got him together and loaded on the back of Minerva the mule, while Mandricardo sputtered something about Braggadocio.

"Can't help it, you know! Poor chap, and all that! Me chivalric duty—fallen comrade! No, it's the bally Burden of the de Malaprops," he stammered excitedly, just before riding off at the best pace Minerva, who was unused to being ridden, could manage. The last they heard of him was the faint echo fading among the bony hills.

"Yoicks! I say, tally-ho! Hark, forrard! *Á Malaprop! Á Malaprop!*"

"Dash it all, hope the old boy gets his Galumphing

Beast!" said Mandricardo feelingly, and he swore by his troth and also by his halidom, whatever those two things are. Just something that knights-errant swear by, I suppose. You've got to swear by something.

When Callipygia made no reply, he peered around and eventually spotted her about thirty feet up the mountain, and climbing rather well, her targe and bow and quiver slung over her back.

"You mind the beasts!" she called down to him.

"Well, I'll be dashed," sighed Mandricardo. What's the use of being a hero, if you're not allowed to act heroically?

Well, never mind . . . *somebody* had to watch the horses.

8

One Teacup Too Many

The front room of the Ogre's castle was about as huge as Mammoth Cave and a lot draftier. Braggadocio sat dispiritedly on the edge of the Ogre's saucer and watched while the huge two-headed brute built a fire (loading in enough tree trunks to make a smallish forest out of), then hung an iron cauldron over the resultant blaze, which he had half-filled with about three thousand gallons of water.*

Into this went all those wainloads of potatoes, carrots, Spanish onions, cabbages, and so forth, and while the basic stock for that night's stew was simmering toward a boil, the Ogre brewed himself a cup of tea and sat down in his chair.

Braggadocio stood on tiptoe and peered into the steaming cup, which was slightly bigger than a garbage can. Seeing all that hot water, faintly tinted with weak tea, made the knight shudder and close

---

* There happened to be a waterfall in the backyard of the Ogre's dwelling.

his eyes. Water in any form was not among Braggadocio's favorite things, and certainly never to be taken internally, if at all possible.

"Gude losh, ye puir oogly brute, hae ye nothing better t' drink than that yon vile, tasteless brew?" he groaned in sympathy, and upended his jug in a toast of commiseration.

The head on the left-hand side of the Ogre's massive torso eyed the jug curiously.

"Whuzzat *yer* drinkin'?" inquired Lefty. Braggadocio cleared his throat, and a crafty glint shone in his canny blue eyes.

"The vurra nectar o' the gods, me gude brute, if ye're innerested in sompling a wee drap . . . ?"

Dexter had just drained the teacup, so the two heads watched with mild interest as Braggadocio upended his jug and stood there while the smoky liquor gurgled slowly into the enormous teacup. It took quite a while to fill the cup, and Braggadocio muttered thankfully under his breath, "A dommed gude thing 'tis *bottomless*, the noo!"

When the cup was filled to the brim with a few dozen gallons of straight *usquebae*, the Ogre took a cautious sip. Dexter drank first, draining half the cup, then sat there smacking his thick blubbery lips, while his eyes watered from the fiery, potent beverage. A tear that consisted of a good quart of salty water trickled down his coarse-pocked cheek to vanish in the bristly thicket of his beard.

Then Lefty finished off the cup, with similar results.

While Braggadocio made haste to fill the cup again, the two heads compared notes with much the air of a duo of wine connoisseurs at a wine-tasting fest.

"*Good*, innit?"

"Berrer'n *'good,'* " Lefty said, judiciously.

Cup after cup followed thereafter, with Bragga-docio taking a sip or two himself, just to be socia-ble. It remains uncertain as to whether Braggadocio had ever heard of the hero Odysseus, who saved his sailors and himself from the appetite of the hungry one-eyed giant, Polyphemus by trampling grapes and getting him drunk on new wine . . . but obviously the minds of heroes tend to think along similar lines.

It was unnerving to watch the Ogre drinking. Obviously, if you stop to think about it, having two heads means that to get much of anything done, you have to learn cooperation. So, the way the monster drank was just this: the right hand took up the teacup and let the left head drink; then the left hand picked up the cup and set it against the lips of the right head; and then vice versa, and so on.

After a while, the Ogre fell off his chair. He sat there on the floor for a time, while beating time on the stone floor with a club made from a huge oak—they were singing a chorus or two of "*Scots wha' hae wi' Wallace bled,*" just then—and finally climbed back into the chair again. Finishing that song, the Ogre regaled Braggadocio with the tra-ditional Ogreish before-dinner song, which goes—

> *Fee, fi, fo, fum,*
> *I smells th' blood uvver Gentlemun!*

and, following that selection, Braggadocio was trying to teach Dexter and Lefty that limerick about the gallant young knight from Cappadocia, when the Ogre fell off the chair again and this time settled down to a good long snooze.

"Foosh, Braggy, me gude mon, but ye're a clever devil! Now t' get oot of here the noo!" said the knight to himself, and began to climb down the leg of the table.

Callipygia put a bold face on it, lady warrior that she was, but as a matter of simple fact, she felt uncomfortable with mountains. Not *looking* at them, you will take my meaning: *climbing* them.

You see, there aren't any mountains on the broad and grassy plains of Pontus, where her homeland is situated, and not even very much in the way of *hills*. And trying to climb up a sheer* cliff of rockface with your targe thumping your hipbone and your quiver of arrows paddling against your behind (and all the while ominous thoughts of landslides, earthquakes and *avalanches* running restlessly through your head), if you aren't used to this hazardous form of exercise, can be a blood-chilling experience.

When she got to the top of the mountain, or, rather, plateau, because the Ogre had built his Den on a flat level mesa sort of thing, she flung herself down in the rock-dust and panted until her heart stopped thumping so painfully against her ribs and the blood stopped singing in her ears.

After a while, she got to her knees and began to reconnoiter. She would gladly have lain there a while longer, just until the muscles in her calves, thighs and forearms stopped jumping, but at any moment, she grimly knew, Sir Braggadocio might be being popped into the bubbling water of the cookpot.

* Well, to *her* it certainly seemed sheer!

. The crack under the front door of the Ogre's castle wasn't wide enough to permit a woman of her rather ample proportions to wriggle under, but, fortunately, on one side of the castle, a mountain pine grew and its uppermost branches just reached to the bottom sill of one of the front windows. And one thing Callipygia *was* good at was climbing trees!

From the top branches she could just peep over the sill into the Ogre's living room, and there he sat, the gross, hideous monster, gloating over his diminutive prisoner, who huddled fearful as a mouse in the shelter of a monstrous cauldron as tall as he was, almost. She did not recognize it, but this was the teacup into which, at the time, Braggy was pouring the liquor from his magic jug. And it seemed to her that the Ogre was gloating horribly ... actually, he was having an attack of the hiccups, but never mind.

"Big bully!" hissed the Amazon girl between clenched teeth.

"I just wish somebody bigger than *you* would come along right about now, and teach you not to pick on people littler than yourself!"

As things would have it, she was restlessly fiddling with that quaint bronze ring she wore on her bicep at the time she muttered this angrily to herself.*

---

* I don't know how to account for the fact, that, even this far into the *Chronicle Narrative* (and Callipygia found the Troll's Ring in the opening chapters of *Mandricardo*), the Amazon princess *still* hasn't stumbled onto the fact that the ring she found in the Troll's cave is a wishing ring. She is really quite intelligent, Callipygia; perhaps the answer lies in the simple fact that, in Terra Magica, many wishes are answered by mysterious forces or personages, and that the granting of a wish is not all that unusual. I don't know.

*   *   *

The Giant Stumbleduffer arose before dawn that
morning, and left his castle atop one of the
Zetzelstein Mountains between the kingdoms of
Orn and Puffleburg quite early. The reason for
that was, quite simply, the larder was empty and
the wolf was at the door. (Well, actually, come to
think of it, no wolf except for one with a yearning
for suicide would come sniffing around a *Giant's*
door, but you know what I mean. Except for half
a ton of ground meal and a few wagonloads of
onions and green peppers, the pantry resembled
an Arctic tundra, except that there is really a lot
more to eat on your common or garden Arctic
tundra.)

And, as he had a yen for elephant stew, did
Stumbleduffer, he headed south across Europe
toward Hindoostan, in whose steaming and tropical jungles elephants of the tastiest variety may
most commonly be found.

Now, do not make the mistake of confusing a
Giant like Stumbleduffer with an Ogre like Grumblegore. Stumbleduffer was a perfectly respectable gentleman Giant, and would not be caught
dead eating Man. Elephant, yes; rhinoceros, sure;
whale, certainly; but—Man? Never! *That* sort of
filthy behavior, Stumbleduffer left, with disdain,
to Ogres and Trolls, and suchlike riffraff.

Humming a little hunting tune under his breath,
in High Giantish, he ambled across the Alps, waded
the Hellespont, and entered Hindoostan. Herds
of wild unicorns stampeded at his approach; co-
bras slithered away from his huge lumbering feet;
monkeys fled, chattering and shrieking; rhinoceri
slunk behind banyan trees, or rhododendron
bushes, or whatever there was to slink behind . . .

because all the jungle knew that the Giant was *hunting*.

And that meant the Giant was hungry.

And when Giants get hungry, they get ... *HUNGRY*.

He carefully avoided trampling over cities, did Stumbleduffer, not only because he was a tender-hearted and really quite civilized sort of Giant,* but also because it is so easy to trip over castles and city walls and fortresses and things, and you can take a nasty fall that way and sometimes do yourself an injury.

This had happened more than once to Stumbleduffer, when he had been younger and more careless, but now the only thing he had tripped over in recent centuries was the occasional smallish sort of Alp or Appenine, and then only on the *most cloudy and moonless* nights.

Wading across the sacred river Ganga, to the dismay of the Gargarids, the horror of the Yogins, the fury of the Brachmans and the calm surmise of the Gymnosophists, he was about to step across a range of hills into his favorite elephant hunting ground, when—and *quite* suddenly, and to the immense amazement of all of the above-listed denizens of Hindoostan, especially including the calmly philosophic Gymnosophists—he vanished like a soap bubble somebody had pricked with a needle.

Braggadocio shinnied down the table leg very much as you or I might shinny down a light pole

---

* Especially when you pause to consider what some of the *other* Giants were like, such as Cormoran and Blunderbore and Corsolt, the Giant of the Brazen Tower, and even his own friend, Thunderthighs, whom we encountered in *Dragonrouge*.

(although we probably wouldn't be wearing bits and pieces of plate armor at the time, no, nor cuddling a precious magic bottomless jug in our bosom).

Reaching the tiled floor, and pausing to restore the tissues once more, and listening to the reassuring, if muted, thunders of the snores of Dexter and Lefty—they snored in counterpoint, as, come to think of it, they *should*—he headed for the front door, the castle stoop, and freedom.

"Ahem! 'Xcuse me! Hello, there?" sounded a deep voice in apologetic tones off to one side, where the enormous cauldron simmered on the roaring hearth.

Braggadocio turned to behold what looked very much like a bird cage, except that it was large enough to hold one very large and muscular man in plate armor, blond hair falling boyishly over his forehead, grinning shyly.

"Oh, gude losh!" groaned Braggy. For he remembered the Ogre's heads, in their desultory conversation, had referred to *another* captive Destined for the cookpot. There was nothing to do but head across the floor of the Ogre's living room, which was big enough to park a fleet of buses in, and head for the cage which stood on the hearth. It was an acre or so distant and took him some little time, and when he came puffing and blowing up to where the younger knight leaned against the bars of the cage, he had to pause to restore his bodily fluids from the contents of the magic jug, before finding breath enough to speak.

"Hello, there," smiled the young knight. "I am hight Sir Blundamore of Beligrance . . . what are you hight?"

Braggy introduced himself, looking the young

man over with an appraising eye. He was certainly
a big one, thought Braggy, and he could not recall
ever before having seen a young man with so
many muscles. Why, he had muscles in places no
one else even had places. Even his muscles had
muscles.

The two put their wits to trying to get Blundamore out of the birdcage, but the iron bars, although rusted rather badly, were the width of
three human fingers, and even all of Blundamore's
strength could not budge them.

They were still trying, when the Ogre woke up
from his nap, and Dexter yawned, and Lefty said:
"Meat's gettin' away, innit?"

9

The Brazen Steed

It didn't take Sir Malaprop very long at all to get himself good and thoroughly lost in the hills, after riding away from his friends in pursuit of the dear Beast. For one thing, the hills all looked exactly like the next, and the little pathways that wound and circled between them were barren of any particular feature, and in no time flat—well, let's say, an hour or two—he gave up.

"Hell's bones," he remarked with feeling, chewing on the butt of an extinct cigar, "had enough of this, dammy!" And, sliding off the back of Minerva the mule, who nudged him gratefully with her warm velvet nose, he took a seat on a convenient hummock, unlatched his helmet, put it down, and plucking a cambric handkerchief from inside his armor, began to swab his streaming brow and face. "Hot work, I must say," he panted. "Ker-hem, dashed if it isn't!"

He felt distinctly sour, and he had every reason so to feel. Two years of bumbling about the world, and not a burble, not a whuffle, not even a bally fewmet, what, from the dashed Beast. And then, just when he had gotten out of that blankety-blanked gaol in Taprobane, and met up with some really fine young people of his own sort, and was about to set out on what had promised to be an entirely new and fascinating sequence of adventures, well, then, at last, at *long* last, up turned the bally Beast, whuffling and bugling to beat the band, and off he had to go—and on a *mule*, mind! —and lose his new friends, and the bally Beast as well.

Heaving a deep sigh, Sir Malaprop relit his dead cigar (using the Ever-Burning Coal he had been given as a Birthday Present by the Enchanter Osmund once, years ago,* and fanned his flushed cheeks with his kerchief.

Then he froze, glimpsing on the hillslope a coppery twinkle.

"Hakk-hem!" he ejaculated, fiddling with his little Ben Franklin type spectacles. No, no question about it: a coppery twinkle. But—from *what*? Coppery twinkles do not just, well, *happen* . . . no, not even here in Terra Magica.

"Well, hell's bones, go and see, what?" mumbled Sir Malaprop to himself, more or less, there being no one else around to hear, unless you care to count Minerva, the mule, who was cropping the rather sparse greenery which was the best these barren hills afforded to hungry mules.

"My word, but I'll just go investigate, what? Hem!" said the fat, bald, elderly, red-faced knight

---

* Which means that Sir Malaprop, who was, as it happens, a True Knight, whatever Sir Braggadocio actually was, had been in Fairyland, as Braggadocio claimed to have been. For this particular Enchanter practiced, ah, enchantery, only in Fairyland.

to himself. "*You'll* be all right, m'dear?" he said, more loudly, addressing Minerva. The mule, flattered to be spoken to, instinctively nodded and went "hee, haw," which charmed Sir Malaprop as much as if he had been addressed by Baalam's ass.

And he got up, putting on his helm, and began— puffingly—to climb the steep hillslope to the cave mouth, wherein that vagrant beam of sunlight had caught and reported to him a Coppery Twinkle.

He entered the dark mouth of the cave.... and I would like for you to *clearly envision this scene.*

We are not talking here about Lancelot or Galahad or even Mandricardo. We are not speaking of a lusty young buck of a knight, a hero in all the vigorous prime of his glorious manhood. Understood? We are talking about an elderly, bald, redfaced old knight named Marmaduke; and we would be well-entitled, by now, to expect him to have long since retired from the pursuit of Galumphing Beasts and careers of knight-errantry, and to have curled up before roaring hearths in comfortable bathrobes and warm carpet slippers, spending the days cozily drinking hot chocolate and writing his Memoirs, not knocking about cold hillsides in heathen lands, hunting for dashed elusive Beasts . . . but, here, I'd better change the subject, for I seem to be falling as much in love with this rather lovable old knight as already has my heroine, Callipygia.

To put it briefly . . . *he found the Brazen Steed.*

Just about the only *good* thing that can be said about having vanished like a pricked soap bubble, is that you frequently reappear. This was the experience of our friend Stumbleduffer a split-second (or so) after the Amazon's wish had snatched him up out of Hindoostan (or whatever passes for Hindoostan in the World Next Door). In brief, he found himself in an entirely different terrain, and directly in his path was a rocky hillcrest, upon which there was builded what could only be an Ogre's Den.

Stumbleduffer regarded it with interest. As he was a trifle nearsighted, as Giants rather tend to be, for some reason, he also regarded it a trifle blurrily, and stepped nearer to the modest edifice* in order to get a clearer look at it.

From within the structure he heard the sounds of voices arguing or squabbling, or something. Two of them were deep bass voices (and as such were probably the voices of Dexter and Lefty), while two others, somewhat higher in pitch and lighter in tone (one of them spoke in a Scots accent you could slice with a butterknife, and simply *had* to be Braggadocio) which meant that the other voice engaged in the heated discussion must have been that of the unknown young knight whom Braggy had gone to the rescue of. If you don't mind my ending a sentence with a mere preposition . . .

Intrigued, Stumbleduffer decided to look in on this scene of multiple argumentation. He did so by the simple feat of lifting the roof off the Ogre's Den, which to one of Stumbleduffer's size and heft was about as easy as you or I might find it to lift the lid off the top of a garbage can.

Nothing, it seems, stops an argument quite as

---

* Of course, it only seemed a modest edifice to the eye of a Giant. You or I would have considered it *huge* . . . unless of course you happen to be a Giant yourself, which does seem unlikely.

swiftly as when the roof of your house is suddenly taken off. Dexter and Lefty gaped upward and blinked; Sir Braggadocio and the other knight stared, their jaws dropping.

"And what," inquired Stumbleduffer in the most severe tones imaginable, "happens to be going on here?" His roving eye did not take long to spot the young knight in the iron cage, or the enormous cook pot, which by now was bubbling and steaming away.

"Oh, nuvvin, Yer Honor," said Dexter, flushing guiltily.

"Thass right, nuvvin!" muttered Lefty.

"Nothin', you say?" demanded Stumbleduffer, in a voice like distant thunder made articulate. A kindly and tenderhearted Giant (as Giants go, of course), Stumbleduffer heartily disapproved of eating Little 'Uns, as he would have put it. This is not to say that the friendly Giant was a vegetarian, in any sense of the word. Of course not—Stumbleduffer certainly had a taste for rhinoceros cutlets, or hippo hash, or elephant stew, or whale steak.

But *Little 'Uns* . . . well, that was another matter. For one thing, it was undignified; for another matter, it tended to give Giants and other Big Folk, like Trolls and Ogres and whatnot, a bad name; and, finally, he deemed the practice unsanitary.

" 'Nothin',' you say?" he repeated, a suspicious glint in his huge and rather nearsighted eyes.

Just then Callipygia rapped on his ankle to get his attention. He peered down with surprise, eyes wandering about, and finally spotted her there in the shadows, no bigger to him than a tiny field mouse would have been to you or me.

"*I'll* tell you what those two great hungry oafs had in mind, Sir Giant!" said our heroine stoutly.

The two heads on the Ogre's broad shoulders
turned to exchange a glance.

"We's in the soup now, Lefty," groaned Dexter.

"Reckon so," sighed Lefty.

Now, while all of these exciting events were occur-
ring atop the mountain in question, Mandricardo
was fuming and fretting below. He had occasion
to reflect sourly that, dash it all, what was the
dashed use of being a dashed knight-errant on an
adventure like this one, dash it all, if you get stuck
with the uninteresting task of tending to the horses?
And you must admit he had a point. But,
then, *somebody* had to take care of Blondel and
Bayardetto—and bony old Rosie—and it might as
well be Mandricardo as anyone else.

After all, as Callipygia is the heroine of this
book, she has to have some adventures, wouldn't
you say, instead of always staying in the background while her Tartar lover did all the fightin'
and gallopin' around and rescuin' and so on?

He could not possibly have missed the fact of
the Giant's sudden appearance, for the huge
shadow of that ponderous form fell over him as
Stumbleduffer melted into existence between
Mandricardo and the sun.

He watched enviously as the Giant lifted the
roof off of the Ogre's Den and he strained his
ears, striving to catch what was being said way up
above him, but could only manage to catch a word
or two, and that only when the breeze happened
to be blowing in his direction. Gnawing fiercely on
the droopy ends of his black mustache, and fond-
ling the hilt of his mighty broadsword, he tried to
figure out if he should not go charging up the
slope to bring his stout blade to the assistance of
his lady-love.

The only thing, really, that deterred him from doing this was a pretty fair notion of what his lady-love would have to say about him horning in on her own personal adventure.

She had a sharp tongue in her head, did Callipygia, for such a well-bred Amazon princess. And she would no doubt have tartly pointed out that, since Mandricardo had already had an entire whole great book written about his adventures,* the least he could do was remain more or less in the background, while she played a leading role in her own book. (This one, I mean.)

So he stayed where he was, chewing vigorously on those poor droopy mustaches of his, which were *never quite the same again*, and all the while wondering silently to himself whatever was going *on* up there in the Ogre's Den.

My Reader may well be wondering the same thing, but I am very much afraid that both he and Mandricardo will have to wait until the next chapter to find out.

---

* My version is called *Mandricardo*, as you might well expect.

10

Introducing Sir Blundamore

It seems that—in Terra Magica, anyway—there was a sort of pecking-order between Giants, Trolls, Ogres, and whatever else there may have been in the way of Very Large People. That is, the bigger you are, the more the smaller of your kindred knuckle under. And Stumbleduffer was a very large Giant: a trifle taller even than his friend, Thunderthighs,* and Thunderthighs was about twenty times as tall as a grown man and tipped the scales at some fourteen tons or so, or would have, anyway, if there had been any scales in Terra Magica big enough to weigh him on.

Keeping these matters in mind, you will not be surprised to learn that Grumblegore the Ogre put up no resistance at all when the Giant sternly bade him set free the Little 'Uns. In fact, Dexter and Lefty were so anxious to get rid of their gigantic, and very uninvited, visitor that they broke

---

* Whom we encountered, you may remember, in Chapter 5 of *Dragonrouge*.

open the cage that held the young knight (whom
we have only been briefly introduced to: his name,
you recall, was Blundamore) and, cradling both
him and Sir Braggadocio gently in their huge
horny palms, handed the two up to Stumbleduffer.

"Now, after this lesson, the two of yez remember t' stick t' eatin' oxen er whativver, ye hear?"
demanded Stumbleduffer sternly, having depos-
ited the two knights and also Callipygia in the
deep pockets of his jerkin, which was as big as a
Barnum & Bailey circus tent. "*No* Little 'Uns, mind!
'Taint fair."

"Yuss," said Lefty, cowed.

"Yuss, *zur*," agreed Dexter.

Mollified, Stumbleduffer replaced the thatched
roof of the Ogre's Den, patting it down nice and
tight again, and then turned about and bore his
pocketful of knights and Amazon down the side
of the mountain. Finding Mandricardo below, arms
akimbo, eyes goggling, he grunted a surly greet-
ing, carefully depositing his burdens before the
Tartar.

Then, knuckling his brow to the lady (a *remarkably*
civil gesture of respect from a Giant, you must
agree), Stumbleduffer turned about and ambled
off into the distance. He stepped over a medium-
sized mountain range as a tall man might step
across a low hedge, and dwindled in the general
direction of Hindoostan, with all those herds of
plump and juicy elephants. . . .

A brief respite after all this excitement in the
cool shade seemed called for, so they retired to a
patch of soft grass under a nearby baobab tree, if
that is really how you spell baobab trees. They
gathered some dry sticks and heated the contents
of Braggy's helm (I should have explained before,

that, always a man concerned with his stomach, before leaving the Ogre's Den, Sir Braggadocio had cleverly filled his helmet with a quart or two of the fragrant vegetable stew that had been bubbling away in Grumblegore's cook pot*), which had cooled off a bit during their descent of the mountain. They enjoyed the tasty stew and perhaps just a jolt or two of the potent contents of Braggy's magic jug.

The young knight, a newcomer to their ranks, was introduced to all. Or, that is, being a knight among knights, he told them what he was hight and they all told him what they were hight, in the approved manner of the knightly heroes in a chivalric romance.

He explained that he was hight Sir Blundamore of Beligrance, and that he had been pursuing a career of knight-errantry chasing around the countryside righting wrongs and rescuing damsels in distress and punishing evil-doers and doing his gosh-darned *best* to battle Wicked Witches, Black Magicians, treacherous Dragons, and suchlike riffraff, when a prominent local member of such riffraff, in the person of Grumblegore, had come upon him while he slept, taken him completely by surprise, snatched him from his bedroll, frightened off his noble—and rather aptly named—snow-white charger, Blanc-Neige, and carried him away to play a rather prominent role in the flavoring of the stew Dexter and Lefty intended to enjoy that evening.

He seemed quite an affable young chap; they looked him over and, on the whole, rather ap-

---

* And which Braggadocio had but narrowly escaped joining as the main ingredient, as seen above.

proved of his appearance. Mention has already
been made of his appearance, to whit that Blundamore was one of those beefy young fellows that
seem literally abulge with muscles. Indeed, he was
so padded with muscle that, had he fallen from a
fairish height, you might easily have expected him
to bounce.

Well, while he did fall down rather often—as
shall very shortly be seen—he did not bounce. He
had yellow hair, forever falling into his eyes, which
were blue and guileless (his eyes, I mean), and
such a fair skin that he seemed perpetually pink
from incipient sunburn. There was something
boyish and enthusiastic and very likable about him.

Callipygia mused: " 'Blundamore' seems like
rather an odd name, sir knight, I must say . . ."

He blushed crimson. "Well, actually, ma'm, it's
more like a nickname; you see, I have this tendency to—"

But actions speak more eloquently than words,
and just then Sir Blundamore blundered into the
fire, knocked over Braggy's helm which had served
them for a cookpot, spilled the rest of the stew,
which, to be honest about it, was almost all gone
anyway, tripped over his own feet, and fell down
with a metallic crash.

All that plate armor, you see.

"Are you hurt, old chap?" demanded Mandricardo, jumping up to offer him a hand. The younger knight grinned sheepishly.

"Oh, no, not at all, thank you, sir! It's just that,
well, I don't know why, but I do always seem to be
bumping into things and knocking them over . . .
it's a *terrible* nuisance, when I happen to be visiting
in a castle, you know. Why, just last winter, I was
staying with King Sagramour le Cote Hardy . . .

he's the one with that fabulous collection of blown-glass ornaments, you know the one I mean?"

Blundamore closed his eyes and shuddered at the memory, which made his armor clink and clank like a cart of tin pots going down a bumpy road.

". . . I wouldn't care to tell you what he doubtless thinks of me to this hour," finished the young knight, with a sigh.

Sir Braggadocio, who was cradling his precious magic bottomless jug against his bosom protectively, with both arms, sternly bade the clumsy youth to stay on *that* side of the clearing.

Having enjoyed a hearty snack from the contents of Braggadocio's battered and rusty helmet, and rested a bit after their recent perils and exertions, the four of them decided that the only thing to do was to comb the countryside, hoping to discover the whereabouts of their lost comrade-in-arms, the redoubtable Sir Malaprop, who had, you will recall, ridden off astride Minerva the mule in quest of the Galumphing Beast.

So Callipygia mounted her mare, Blondel, and Mandricardo ascended to the saddle of his great black charger, Bayardetto, while Braggadocio, rendered supple and lissome due to several potent quaffings from the bottomless black jug, slithered into Rosie's saddle and professed himself ready for any adventure.

They rode off in the direction taken by Sir Malaprop, and, erelong, the medium-sized mountain, atop which stood the Ogre's Den, fell astern and dwindled in what, so to speak, you might call their wake, if you were of a nautical bent.

Since he had no steed, and was much too

burly and beefy to share one of their own with one of them, Sir Blundamore perforce had to walk. But the huge blond youth was so agreeable and good-natured that he professed most earnestly that he found it no great hardship, especially, he added, after being pent in that iron cage for so long. His legs were cramped, he explained, and he wished for nothing more than to stretch them with a bit of exercise.

As they rode, and he walked, the knights talked about . . . well, about whatever it *is* that knights talk about, when they are alone amongst themselves: quests and heraldry and jousts and stuff, I suppose; lance oil and saddle wax; and buckle polish, and, for all I know, vambraces and greaves and gorgets and couters and pauldrons and cuisses* and like that.

Also—since he proved to be an eager and enthusiastic audience—they told Sir Blundamore about some of their recent adventures. About the Wandering Garden and the Troll's Cave and how they had acquired the Magic Flying Carpet, and how Mandricardo had cleverly tricked the deadly Salamandre into picking a quarrel with the equally deadly Undina, causing both to vanish in a mushroom cloud of superheated steam,* and about some even earlier adventures, when they had set free the Red Dragon, and petrified the Egyptian wizard Zazamanc by turning back upon him his own

---

* These are parts of a suit of plate armor. We fantasy writers have to know all about these things, you know.

* Since the elemental spirits of Fire and Water mutually cancel each other out . . . but you can read all about these matters in *Mandricardo*, if you like, and I hope you do, for I can use the royalties.

basilisk-spell, and how they had tricked a Genie or
two, and . . . well, there was quite a lot to tell. And
I have no doubt, or very little, but that Sir Blundamore found it all highly edifying and educational.

For his own part, Sir Braggadocio told them a
very colorful and somewhat confused narrative of
marvels, most of which you or I would recognize
as having been borrowed from the *Faerie Queene*
and the *Orlando Furioso* and other romances, except that in Terra Magica, of course, they are not
romances at all, but serious and sober works of
history. He got all the names mixed up, and fell
off his bony, ambling steed more than a time or
two, as to relieve the tedium of their journey he
had been surreptitiously taking the ever and occasional sip of his favorite potent beverage from the
bottomless black jug.

Between the musical crashing of armor, when
Sir Blundamore fell over a cactus or whatever,
and the more resonant jangling of armor, when
Sir Braggadocio fell off his bony steed, their meandering journey was punctuated by an odd, sort
of atonal music.

And "meandering" was the perfect word for it.
These mountainy parts, around Grumblegore's
Den, consisted of nothing else but dry and dusty
ravines that wove in and out and about between
rocky outcroppings and stony hillocks and suchlike. It took them the time it would have taken, on
the straightaway, to go half a mile to travel two,
what with all these meanderings. Finally, Callipygia
announced that she had had enough. And the
Amazon girl suggested they mount the Magic Flying
Carpet, which now bore their baggage, and command it to take them—in, say, three installments—to
the other side of these mountains, where perhaps

they would be fortunate enough to find *a lush and fertile plain of dewy verdure,* as the romances of chivalry always describe such.

This they wasted no time in doing, since they were all by this point heartily sick and tired of weaving in and out of curving mountain roads. First the Carpet flew Callipygia and Blondel due east, depositing her on a verdant plain beyond the high country, then Braggadocio and his bony nag, Rosie, finally Mandricardo and Bayardetto and the newest addition to their number, the amiable if clumsy Sir Blundamore.

Rolling up the Carpet and stowing it away in their gear (once it had shrunk itself back to ordinary carpet size, of course), the Tartar knight looked about at the plush meadows with a gleam of satisfaction in his dark eye.

"Dash it all, Cally, but this is more like, what?" he positively chirped. Without waiting for invitations, the three horses moved out and began to crop *the dewy sward*; the Amazon girl plucked a ripe pear from laden boughs overhead and began to munch placidly; Braggadocio tripped over a hummock and fell to earth with a jingling thump, curled up under a rhododendron bush and began to snooze just a little.

The day had worn on, as days always do, and what with all they had been through, our heroes may be forgiven if the hour proved later than they would have thought. Already the west was a magnificence of gold and purple pomp, like the funeral of an emperor, and night birds were arrowing across skies of darkening amethyst.

The Amazon girl open her mouth to make some remark, perhaps a sentimental observation, on the beauty of early evening or whatever-it-would-have-been, then uttered a shriek, sprang to her feet, and clutched the nearer of her weapons, pointing wordlessly with her other hand. Mandricardo sprang to his feet, ripping off a manly oath in High Tartar, I suppose, and stared in amazement.

As there advanced upon them the most frightful and remarkable monster . . . or do I, perhaps, mean *contraption?*

BOOK THREE

Sorcery
in
Sangaranga

11

Of Cambuscan and Other Celebrities

Now, let me see if I can do justice to this scene of dramatic confrontation:

Sky an arching vault of gold and purple, right; previously noted. Horses gratefully gobbling away at dewy sward. Three knights lolling about, Amazon nibbling pear. Cool breezes of early evening (not previously mentioned, but there, of course, given the hour and the climate). Everywhere peace and tranquillity. And *then*—

A clatter, a clanking, a banging, the buzzing and whirring, as of some infernal clockwork mechanism purring away within a hollow metallic space.

Dying sunlight flashes, sparkling, from a moving object—or monstrosity—with *a coppery twinkle*!

High atop this fantastic creature, who is relentlessly pounding down upon them, sits a small figure waving and hallooing and crying out things like "Tally ho!" and "Yoicks!" and "I say, you fellows, what ho!"

It looked rather like a horse, in that it seemed to be designed along lines more horselike than not. But the thing was considerably larger than a horse, more like a camel or even one of the smaller elephants of Hindoostan and it moved—or perhaps I should say, *progressed?*—with a sort of stately mechanical gait that went very well with the clatter of the purring clockwork inside its hollow shell.

It was a Horse of Brass, a jointed mechanical creature, obviously animated by some powerful spell of magic; there on the saddle horn you could see the knobs and the wheel which controlled its speed and direction. The brass wherefrom it was made was old, very old, and very badly needed polishing: green and dingy and dim with verdigris it was, but Sir Malaprop had not taken with him when he had ridden off in all directions after the Galumphing Beast his lance polish and saddle oil and other knightly things, and so could only give the Brazen Steed* a rough brush up and a lick and promise.

Spying them through his dim spectacles, he waved both hands frantically, semaphoring. "What ho, you fellows! Hem! and Mistress Cally, of course! Well, I say, what? Here we all are, together again— who's that new felly, one who just fell over the tree root, what?—'arf a mo', I'll turn the brute off if I can find the right knob . . . kaff! Not *that* one; hem, ah, there we go!"

With a rattle, a wheeze, and a piercing series of squeaks, the Brazen Steed subsided to immobility

---

* I remember, in an earlier book in this sequence, I referred to some article both as "brass" and as "brazen," and found myself taken to task by an alert but less-than-literate reader, who objected that "brazen" refers to bronze. But *brazen* does not refer to bronze, it refers to anything made of *brass*. My dictionary is the Random House College Dictionary, edition of 1984, and it can wrastle *your* dictionary to the mat two falls out of three. Betcha.

in mid-stride, so to speak, which made him—her?
—it?—just a bit lopsided, but never mind. They
assisted Sir Malaprop down from the very high
saddle, thumping him on his armored back and
shoulders and crying knightly greetings and suchlike, which I will not bother to repeat here, and
then craned back to admire the fabulous anti-
quity, the historical treasure. For in Terra Magica,
you must be given to understand, the Brazen Steed
occupies a position more or less one with the *Ti-
tanic*, or the *Spirit of St. Louis*, or . . . well, I can't
quite say *what*.

"Dash it all, what?" breathed Mandricardo rev-
erently, craning his neck, staring at the noble arched
back, where carefully carved brass curls emulated
the crisp mane of a real horse.

"Quite right, m'boy," whispered Sir Malaprop.

"After all these years," murmured Callipygia.

"Generations," said the Tartar, absently.

"Hell's bones—*centuries!*" said Sir Malaprop
with feeling. Just then, I am afraid to say, Sir
Blundamore, staring up at the towering shape of
sparkling (more or less sparkling, you understand)
metal, backed up to get a better view and tripped
in his usual way over one of the immense hooves
of the Horse of Brass and fell with a resounding
crash of armor on the ground.

He also, as it happened, fell on Sir Malaprop's
left foot, and the elderly knight, turning purple as
a turnip,* began leaping and hopping about in a
little circle, nursing his injured extremity.

"Oh, blankety-blank the blankety-blanked blank,
dash it all!" he cursed. Eventually Sir Blundamore

---

* Or do I mean a beet? Isn't one or the other of them purple?
Well, no matter—on with my scene.

shamefacedly assisted the older man to a comfy
hummock and begged his pardon. As for Malaprop, he also looked a bit shamefacedly in the
direction of Callipygia.

"Ker-hem! Par'm my Egyptian Hieroglyphic,
ma'm!"

"You're par'med, I'm sure," smiled our heroine.

The others, paying little attention to this, were
staring up, rapt in admiration, with awe stirring in
their several hearts, as the rich glory of the gloam-
ing gleamed and glimmered on the tarnished shoulders and flanks and smoothly-jointed and cunning-
ly-articulated limbs of the mighty, the magnificent, Horse of Brass.

"Drop or two of buckle polish an' a little elbow
grease'll soon put that tarnish to rights, and have
him shining again, ker-haff!" Sir Malaprop assured them with a proud, proprietary glisten in
his eye.

Whichever master magician it had been who had
cunningly fabricated the Brazen Steed* was no
longer remembered of men. But it had been the
Grand Prince of the Indies who had dispatched
the Knight of the Mirror upon the Brazen Steed
to the court of the celebrated Cambuscan, emperor of Tartary, and one of Mandricardo's own
ancestors, more-or-less.

"Came bearin' gifts and a marriage-proposal to
Princess Canace, don't you know," said Mandricardo
offhandedly. It made him redden to seem to be
boasting about his more famous relatives. "Came

---

* And it suddenly occurs to me to wonder if, after all, it might not
have been the famous firm of Smith & Tinker, before they relocated to the Moon? See the Notes.

to Sarray, I think it was—our winter capital in those days, what. Interrupted a feast, I seem to remember. Studied it all in school, you know, but, dash it all, that was years ago!"

The Amazon girl looked dreamy, chin resting in one cupped palm. "There was a love letter from the Indian prince," she murmured, "and the gifts included a magical sword of some sort and the famous mirror, and a ring—"

"Ker-hem!" sniffed Sir Malaprop. "Dashed *mirror* showed old Cambuscan visions of future adversities, invasions, calamities, whatever. Sounds like a useful gadget to have about the castle."

"Studied it all in school meself, you know," he added.

"Yes, and the ring, well, you put it on your thumb or in your purse or pocket or whatever," said Mandricardo, for it was all coming back to him now, "and you could understand the speech of birds."

They looked at him.

"*Birdies,* ye say, the noo?" demanded Braggadocio incredulously (having just awakened from the most recent installment of his nap, rejoining them in mid-discussion of the Steed, as it were).

"Birds," said Mandricardo flatly. Then, as they continued to stare at him in a rather puzzled fashion, "Well, dash it all, you chaps, don't blame me! So my tutors—ah—tutored me."

"Haff!" muttered Sir Malaprop, cleaning his spectacles briskly on a fine silk handkerchief. "Wonder why 'birds'? Shouldn't think the little chappies 'd have very much to say that anybody'd really want to hear, even if you *could* understand what all that twitterin' and chirpin' and miscellaneous noise meant . . ."

The Tartar knight shrugged, growing slightly irritable, as if by questioning this curious fact of ancient Tartar history, his comrades were somehow making him look foolish.

"Dashed if *I* know! Maybe Canace was downright crazy about birds, what? I say—time to put on the old feedbag, eh?"

And so Sir Malaprop gained a steed fitting to his rank and lineage, and a fine steed it was, if you could put up with all the whirring and clicking of its magical interior clockwork mechanism.

It was indeed dinnertime, and our friends divided the various evening tasks between them. While Sir Blundamore scrounged through the trees, picking up dry branches for the cookfire and only once or twice falling over a bush or log or somewhat tripping over a tree root, Callipygia ranged the verdant plain—*love* that phrase!—and, with her unerring eye and excellent sense of bowmanship (bowmanry? There must be some word that means what I am trying to say, but let's get on with the narrative) and, erelong, returned to their camp with a brace of fat pheasants, or perhaps they were wild turkeys. None of them were any too familiar with the fauna of these Eastern parts, so none could say for sure: not that it mattered particularly. They proved to be quite delicious when broiled over a crackling slow fire . . .

While the hunting and wood-gathering had been going on, Malaprop and Mandricardo and, later, Blundamore, had busied themselves cleaning up and refurbishing the Brazen Steed. Just as the elderly knight had so confidently predicted, a drop or two of buckle polish, perhaps half a jigger of lance oil, and plenty of elbow grease soon restored the shine and sparkle of the coppery creature, until by suppertime he flashed and glittered in the light of their cookfire no less resplendently than, ages before, he had appeared when making his stately and historic entrance at the court of Cambuscan.

Braggadocio, seated comfortably in his lawn chair and clad in his red flannel long underwear, refreshing himself from time to time from that little black jug of his, gave the polishers the benefit of his wise advice and keen-eyed perceptiveness.

"Joost a *leetle* more to the left, me gude mon, ah, that's it! Lay into it, now ... ah, gude losh, makes all the deeferince in the world, d'ye ken?"

"Lazy beggar," breathed Sir Malaprop under his breath, as he puffed and polished.

"Let him be," grinned Mandricardo sympathetically. "In his condition, dash it all, he'd be no use to us at all ..."

They ate dinner under the splendid stars of Asia, and slept the sleep of the weary, and the just, bundled in blankets about the coals of the dying fire, except for Mandro and Cally, who slept in their pavilions.

The next morning, after a breakfast composed largely of the scraps and remnants of the gamebirds they had dined on the night before, leavened with some fresh fruit they had discovered in the little wood—odd Oriental fruits, I should imagine,* you know the sort of thing I mean, breadfruit or melons or figs or guavas or dates or avocados or mangoes or whatever—they mounted up and rode on.

* The *Chronicle Narrative* does not specify.

Since they had come this far east, it seemed a lot easier to Braggadocio to continue on with them, rather than to try to turn back now and make it all the long, long way back to Caledonia on his own. And, after all, since he had last decided to head back home, he had been carried off by the Ogre, and now there were all these mountains in the way . . . and where some mountains happen to be home to a man-eating Ogre and, if not home, at least occasionally visited, by a Galumphing Beast, who can say what other fearsome or dangerous creatures might haunt their heights and steeps and clefts?

Or, as Sir Braggadocio put it in his own inimitable, if rather rambling, mode of speech: "Whurra, gude sor and moddom, an' friends old an' new, ye've a pairfect right to ken the whole sorra business. But we've gone sae far sae gude togither, and, findin' meself far, far fra' hame, where better to spend th' gert winter, with its rheumatiz and sciaticks and cheelbains, too, that before a gert roarin' fire in some snug castle o' Tartary? A gude, long rest durin' th' cold weather and the gert frosts o' Tartary, and, ah-weel, with spring mayhops I'll be thinkin' o' the long rode back to me ain hame—with the help on yon cunnin' Carpet, it might be, gude sor—"

"Well, dash it all, I say!" huffed and whuffed Mandricardo, behind his own mustache, which, if not the bristly red walrus sort sported by his Caledonia colleague, was still a notable item of hirsute facial adornment, after all. It was not at all to the liking of the Tartar prince that the Magic Flying Carpet (which would be, you must understand, quite an adornment to *any* kingdom for half the world around, as how many kingdoms have Magic

Flying Carpets in their treasuries or museums?)
should stray from Tartarean hands.

But these, of course, were matters that could be
discussed later on, in the spring say, months from
now.

They rode on, chatting amongst themselves. The
Steed of Brass was so huge—big as a camel, as I
have remarked, and even taller—that there was
room aboard the glittering mechanism for Sir
Blundamore, who was quite grateful not to have
to walk afoot any more. After all, when you are
crossing Asia, it is easier and more comfortably
done aboard a vehicle or steed of one kind or
another, than on what they used to call shanks'
mare.

During this leg of their journey it somehow
seemed only natural for them to let Sir Malaprop
and his illustrious (and also, now that it was highly
polished, *lustrous*) Steed take the lead, with the
rest of their company trailing after, Minerva and
the Carpet laden with their luggage bringing up
the rear.

Neither Bayardetto nor Blondel *approved at all*
of their new four-footed colleague. For one thing,
the creature, while horselike to the eye, did not
smell of horse—nor of anything else their nostrils
could detect, except a little graphite and some
metal polish, not to mention machine oil. And,
while horses do not depend as much on their
sense of smell to identify other creatures as, ah,
um, other creatures do, still and all, when you are
confronted by immense and unknown and glittering metallic creatures which purport to be horses,
you employ every sense you have on hand to help
sort the creature out.

For another thing, they did not at all like the

way its innards hummed and buzzed, clicked and purred, whizzed and clacked and whirred, and made other annoying clockworky noises designed, it seems, to unsettle horses usually phlegmatic. After trying to manage the recalcitrant brutes for a time, Mandricardo and his Amazonian lady-love quite sensibly let their steeds fall back a bit until they had put a comfortable little piece of distance between themselves and the enormous gleaming brassy creature that looked like a horse but neither smelled nor sounded like one. Whereupon the horses became more tractable and cantered along, giving their master and mistress no more trouble.

Except for Braggy's bony old nag, Rosie. She just plodded along, no matter what was happening, dreaming of Food. Food was the only thing that interested her, and Steed of Brass or no Steed of Brass, lunchtime was somewhere up ahead rather soon, and that was, as I have said, the only thing that could stir Rosie from her usual state of numb boredom, or apathy, or whatever you might care to call it. Would lunch consist of moist, lush meadow grass this time, or dry, crunchy thistles? A nosebag of luscious kernel corn, or ripe barley, or wheat? Would there perhaps be a raw apple after lunch, or a juicy carrot, or even a turnip?

Hers was a simple life, was Rosie's, and with simple needs. And most of these could be summed up under the general heading of . . . *lunch*.

12

Welcome to the Poorest Kingdom

Along about midmorning, our party of travelers found the ground rising into barren and rocky hills, and followed the meandering road which led to the nearest pass therethrough.

Here they found themselves confronted by a roadsign. It was old and weathered, and hanging by only one rusty nail, and the paint was scaling away in strips, but it could still be read.

WELCOME TO SANGARANGA!

it read ... but some other hand had scrawled a morsel of commentary, or perhaps warning, underneath this legend, to wit:

*Go there only if you
have nowhere else to go!*

They looked at one another in silence for a time; Braggadocio puffed on his reeking briar, scratched

bestubbled cheeks, and took a surreptitious nip
from his little black jug; Malaprop ker-hemmed!
and hak-kaffed! and polished his little spectacles
so vigorously on his fine silk handkerchief that it
was a wonder he did not polish them away into
nothingness; Mandricardo tugged on the droopy
ends of his fine black Tartar mustache, and eyed
the sign dubiously.

"I say you chaps, what? Anybody know anything about this Sangaranga?" he inquired.

Callipygia shrugged: these further parts of Asia
were unknown to the Amazon girl. "Never heard
of the place, meself, hem!" said Sir Malaprop.
Then Sir Blundamore spoke up.

"Might be something about it in my Gazetteer,"
said the amiable, muscle-bound youth.

"Oh, you have a Gazetteer?" said
Callipygia, surprised. The young knight grinned
and shrugged, knocking over what little was left
of the sign which pointed—*had* pointed—down
the pass to Sangaranga.

"Only thing left of my luggage, when the two-
headed Ogre frightened off poor Blanc-Neige,"
he said, picking of the sign apologetically, dusting
it off, and propping it against the side of the pass.
"Have it here somewhere . . . let me see. . . ."

He dug around under his cuirass and came up
with a fat volume bound in limp leatherette.
Callipygia peered curiously at the title, which was
in gold lettering. It covered almost all of the cover
of the book and, for all she ever knew, was continued on the back cover, for it was just about the
longest book title that the Amazonian princess had
ever seen or even heard of.

Noticing her interest in it, the nice young knight
held it up for all to see.

"Happened to be browsing through it when the Ogre snatched me up for his, or their, cookpot," he explained. "Picked it up in Samarkand, I think it was, or perhaps Basrah. Thought a Gazetteer would be a handy thing to have along on a journey into the East, you understand, sort of give you advance warning as to what you might be getting into . . ."

The title was:

Gazetteer of the More Interesting and Renowned Realms to be Found in the Hithermost Parts of the East of Terra Magica, as Compiled and Selected from the Most Approved and Respected and Pertinent Texts, for the Use of the Cautious and Prudent Traveler, and Now Newly Edited and Arranged by the Most Noted Scholars, Geographers and Authorities—

"Oh, gude losh," said Braggadocio irritably. "Git on with it, laddie! D'ye ken if it has nowt to say aboot Sangarangy?"

"Certainly, let me see, now," muttered Sir Blundamore, leafing hurried through the pages, and only ripping two or three in the process ". . . now let me see, Sarray in Tartary, Sarras—ah, here we are! 'Sangaranga: Smallest and quite possibly the poorest of all the countries of Hithermost Asia, long plagued by wicked magicians, and notable only for,' " and here he rattled off the usual list of tourist views, historical sites, the occasional statue of Amadis or Tirante the White or Orlando, all of whom had wrought heroic wars and deeds and exploits in these Easterly parts.

Mandricardo looked dubiously at his lady-love. "What d'you think, Cally? Give it a try? How bad can the place be, what?"

"I suppose we might at least ride through," she said without any noticeable enthusiasm.

"Rather fun, you know, crossing lances with a wicked magician or what-have-you," added Mandricardo a bit wistfully. It still smarted that Callipygia had enjoyed the leading role in the last adventure, against the two-headed Ogre, while he had been left at the bottom of the mountain to tend to the horses. A good bout with a wicked magician was just what the Tartar knight needed to life his spirits.

Braggadocio was snoozing and swaying in the saddle, humming "*Scots wha' hae*" under his breath— which was by now potent enough to paralyze wasps at ten paces, had there been any wasps around to be paralyzed—so he didn't care. To visit Sangaranga was perfectly all right with Sir Malaprop, and Blundamore cheerfully agreed that one road was all the same as another, to him.

So they went down the pass to Sangaranga, the poorest kingdom in the world. . . .

And the place certainly lived up to its advance billing. There was only one city, well, more of a *town*, really, with a dusty white road leading into it and another dusty white road leading out of it, and a small sluggish river went trickling and gurgling by underneath a rickety bridge or two, heavily laden with hungry-looking fishermen who hung over the water, their hooks trailing in the stream, avidly watching for the smallest minnow to come swimming by. Seeing how eagerly they hunched over the water, scrutinizing every wavelet, you got the impression that if, by some miracle, a fat trout or river-salmon should come by, half the fishermen would fling themselves bodily into the stream to seize the prize. (And you would not have been wrong, either.)

They approached the city through dismal clumps of rather motheaten date palms and there were also some dusty and poorly-irrigated orange groves. Passing through a stand of dilipidated fig trees and a couple of listless olives, they found scrawny peasants apathetically hoeing in scruffy patches of dry earth where grew, more or less, cabbages, leeks, turnips, and other unappetizing but nourishing groceries. These farmers stopped work as the procession passed by, leaning on their hoes (many of which were broken and were only held together by bits of twisted wire or stout twine), observing the strangers without very much curiosity.

"Wonder if they think they're being invaded?" giggled the Amazon princess to Sir Malaprop. The elderly knight, perched high atop the magnificent Steed of Brass, hemmed and kaffed, then grinned and observed that they were probably hopeful that they were. "After all, me gel, invaders have to feed they subjects, you know . . . if only to back up they investment! Hell's bones, look at that—!"

They had come into full view of the little city, or largeish town, whichever would be the more correct, and could see it plain. Like most Oriental cities, it was built in a square and had a wall around it of dressed stone which had once, years and years ago, been plastered. Most of the plaster had peeled off it by now and one whole side of the city wall had fallen down and stood about in moldering heaps of rubble, thickly-grown with thistles, nettles and rank weeds.

The guard stationed at the gate awoke from a nap under his awning to take their entrance fee. The gates themselves were missing and had probably long since been sold to junkmen for the scrap bronze. The only coins Mandricardo had on him

were those gold dinars he had obtained much
earlier in his adventures, when he had cashed in a
pigeon's-blood ruby.

The guard eyed it suspiciously, bit it a time or
two, and showed it to his captain, who came yawning and scratching from the courtyard, where he
had been frying onions. The two muttered over
the coin, their heads together, and finally decided
to accept it—"But no change, mind you, yer honor!"

It was then that it dawned upon our travelers
that the Sangarangians had not seen a bit of gold
in such a long time that they had almost forgotten
what the stuff looked like, and what it was good
for.

"Oh, raw-*ther!* No change needed," said Mandricardo agreeably. "I say, old chap, can you direct
us to the nearest caravanserai?"

The captain of the guard scratched himself again,
as if by this form of stimulus to accelerate the
mental processes.

"Well, stranger . . . Abdullah's place is the only
inn left open, so it'll have to do yer, dump though
it be!" He cocked a callused thumb easterly.
"Through the bazaar, yer'll see it on 'tother side."

They rode through the town, and those like Sir
Malaprop and Sir Blundamore, who were new to
these exotic Eastern realms, gawked at the various
spires and minarets and at the huge onion-shaped
copper domes. They tried not to notice the scrawny
beggars picking through last week's garbage, the
naked urchins trying to catch pigeons in traps of
twine, the clumps of weed growing up through
holes in the crooked streets, where cobblestones
were missing, or how many of the huts, houses
and hovels were falling down, or already had.

The bazaar was an even more pathetic spectacle.

There was hardly anything for sale worth the selling, just cracked earthenware pots, chipped cups and dishes, a few dented tin pots and pans and a few threadbare, faded, muchly-patched articles of clothing. The grocer, however, was thriving—well, *relatively* thriving. It seems he had been up well before dawn, raiding the marshy banks of the little sluggish river, and had fetched back to market a modest fortune in plover's eggs which were going like hotcakes.

The inn was as rundown as the rest of the town, but Abdullah the innkeeper was so pathetically eager for actual paying customers that they did not (as they decided on first glance) turn away, but figured it was the least they could do to boost the sagging local economy to stay on for lunch.

Having groomed, fed and watered their steeds—for the inn could no longer afford to keep and feed a stableboy, and had sold the last one to the gypsies—they sat down at a trestle table and tried to work up some enthusiasm for lunch.

"I say, innkeeper, what!" chirped Mandricardo, burbling with false heartiness, trying to cheer up the woeful-looking Abdullah. "What's on the bally menu for luncheon, eh?"

"The specialty of the day, yer honor, is a loverly barley gruel, served up with a garnishin' of stewed leeks and sliced cabbitch ... unless yer honor'd prefer what do be left over fum *yestiddy's* specialty of the day, which were potato skins simmered in vinegar, with goat cheese on the side and fresh watercress. Fresh *yestiddy*, that is. Got some date wine, too. Beginning to turn bad, so it's goin' at bargain rates ..."

The travelers exchanged eloquent glances of commiseration, but they were already here and couldn't just up and leave (which would not at all have been the *knightly thing to do*), so Mandricardo, rolling his eyes heavenward and heaving a gusty sigh, ordered everything on the menu and offered to pay extra for a brace of those plover's eggs for sale down in the bazaar, if any were left.

Some were, and something resembling an edible omelette was eventually served to assuage the hunger of the travelers.

After lunch, they ambled about, exploring and seeing such sights as there were to see, and there wasn't much.

"Whatever do you suppose happened here?" murmured Callipygia.

"A-weel," grumbled Braggadocio, gnawing thoughtfully on the ends of his walrus mustache, " 'tisloike they be laborin' under a curse, d'ye ken, moddom? The lond looks peerfectly a-richt, ye ken, but beyond a doot they're cairtainly bein' drained dry (the puir feelthy heathen louts!) by some wicked sorcery or 'tother— but, oh, deary me, I've ha' me doots that there be nowt that we can do will sairve!"

"They'd be able to tell us up at the palace, ker-heff!" said Sir Malaprop pertly.

They decided to follow his suggestion.

13

About Alibeck the Avaricious

The King of Sangaranga was named Akbad, and he was short and stout and bald, under an enormous turban of faded silk covered all over with glittering jeweled pins and brooches. It was only upon closer scrutiny that you could see that these ornamentations were nothing but bits of colored glass or cheap paste in thin gilt or pinchbeck settings.

He had bristling white whiskers and was so affable and welcoming that they tried not to notice how the ceilings of his palace were cracked and some of the wall hangings torn and faded, and that more than a few of the floor tiles were loose underfoot in the throneroom, and that his best ermine robe, which he had obviously hastily donned in their honor, needed mending along the fringe.

King Akbad greeted them effusively, and not at all for the same reason that the innkeeper, Abdullah, had been so happy to see them. No, it was not the possible influx of coinage which the kingdom might acrue from their presence which so excited

the stout little monarch, as the fact that they were
a hardy band of chivalric and noble-hearted
knights-errant (and lady-errant, or whatever-it-was
that we should consider Callipygia to be), and that
his was a poor little kingdom badly in need of a
spot or two of knight-errantry!

They were at once invited to a banquet in their
honor that very evening—although, as they later
learned, the Castle Cook squawked, rolled up her
eyes in her head, and fainted dead away on the
spot upon learning that there were *five* of them to
feed, not counting the King.

This particular banquet was . . . well, to be
honest, they had, each and every one of them,
enjoyed more sumptuous viands at picnics along
the road during their various adventures. But since
King Akbad seemed so pathetically proud of the
meager best his table could afford, in all the poverty of his realm, to lay before his honored guests,
they set their private feelings aside and feasted
with many a polite murmur of appreciation.

The dinner began with a thin slice of pink melon
set before each of them, and this was followed by
cracked plates upon which reposed, in lonely splen-
dor, three dry sardines each, centered on a lettuce
leaf.* This was, in turn, followed by the soup dish,
which was a potato soup, thick and creamy, and
certainly *nourishing*, if not exactly a gourmet's delight. Then came the main dish, a sort of casserole
of hot buttered parsnips and turnips—and poor
Mandricardo, who *simply hated parsnips*, gritted his
teeth, grimly recalled to mind his knightly oath,
and manfully chomped his way through the mess.

---

* The *Chronicle Narrative* underscores the fact that it was *one*
lettuce leaf each. Oh, Sangaranga was *poor*, all right!

Dessert was ripe figs, dates, nuts (the chamberlain, by a fluke, had fortunately discovered at the *very last minute* half a bushel of last fall's walnuts hidden away in the cupboard, so they had that unexpected treat. This rather Spartan repast was washed down, thankfully—not with the turning-bad date wine of the inn, which had given several of them a slight queasiness of the tummy*—but with the dregs of a rather good brew of strong black ale which King Akbad had been saving for a day when there was something to celebrate.

After the dishes had been cleared away, as they sat around munching on a few rather wrinkled and over-ripe local apricots, and crunching the chewy walnuts, they broached the matter of the poverty of the kingdom. Akbad, mellowed by the unfamiliar experience of playing host to visiting foreign gentry, by their appreciation for his bounty, and by the conversational sallies that had hurled across the cutlery during the meal, was in a relaxed and talkative mood.

"Ah, yes! Weren't always this poor, ye know! Certainly not," he sighed. "Silver mines in the mountains, smaragdines in the hills; good crops; lambs, goats ... not *rich*, mind you, but comfy enough. Look at us now, eh? Dashed kingdom's so poor we could only afford to keep one city, forced to sell off the other to the kingdom next door* some years back ..."

---

* Not including, of course, our friend Sir Braggadochio, who declined the beverage, saying, "Thank ye, but noo, I ha' me ain refrashmints wi' me—puirly on the advice o' me physician, ye wull onderstond."

* The *Chronicle Narrative*, rather archly, remarks that this kingdom was "aptly named Nexdoria." I deplore cheap puns, don't you? Not that this one is all that bad ...

"You sold off one of your *cities?*" blinked Mandricardo incredulously. The stout little monarch shrugged helplessly.

"Had to, young feller! Only had two in the kingdom, anyway. Couldn't afford to keep up th' two of 'em, you know. Why, the upkeep and repairs and maintenance on the roads alone . . . *or* the bridges. And, as for the blasted *drains* . . . wellsir! D'ye have any idee what plumbers charge by the hour in these benighted days?"

They let the question pass, and asked him how things had managed to get themselves in such a sorry state as this. He looked mutinous and plucked fiercely at his bristly white whiskers.

"Hired meself this new Grand Vizier, feller name of Alibeck," the King admitted. "Had to; last one ran off with the wife of the ambassador from—well, *thet's* neither here nor there! Anyway . . . feller had the best credentials, and his references were impeccable! Kingdom of this, dukedom of that, barony of the other place . . . ah, the rogue, the rascal, the—"

A knowing light flashed in Mandricardo's dark eye.

"I say, Akbad, old chap, this wasn't a vile cad and bounder known as Alibeck *the Avaricious*, was he? Because if it was, well, I've heard tales about the bounder that would curl your hair. . . !"

Akbad heaved a mountainous sigh. "None other than the very rogue," he confessed mournfully. "Should have checked the blighter's references. Blame meself, you know. The buck stops here, as the feller said."

"Ker-heff!" sniffed Sir Malaprop. "Pray continue, sire!"

"Well, things went along smoothly enough for a

time. Then my new Grand Vizier suggested he take over the job of Royal Tax Collector, saying he could handle both positions easily enough and the realm would save itself an extra salary. Seemed a good enough idea to *me*. Anything to save a pazool. That's our local coinage, you know, or mebbe you don't know. Dashed few of them you'll see around here, I fear. Pazools." He fell into a moody silence, apparently pondering upon the inscrutable and elusive currency problems.

Callipygia cleared her throat. "Pray continue, Your Majesty," she suggested.

The little monarch roused himself from his brown study, and heaved a sigh. "Quite right, quite right!" he said gruffly. "I'll see what I can do to make a long story short, for after a feast like the one *we* just finished—whoof!" He patted his stout little round belly. "Well, we'll all be wantin' our beds before too long—"

Mandricardo was about to guffaw quite rudely, when he caught the fierce commanding eye of his Amazon lady-love on him, purpled, strangled the guffaw into a *harrumph*. Nevertheless, dash it, he *did* think it was amusin' that King Akbad considered the meager repast he had just set before them as something remotely resembling a feast. Why, the Tartar knight had enoyed more sumptuous meals in gaol, more than once!

But the King had picked up the threads of his narrative. "Anyway," King Akbad was saying, "it turned out soon enough this Grand Vizier of mine was none other than a Wicked Wizard—"

"No! I say!" blurted Blundamore, knocking over his goblet.

"—A Wicked Wizard," repeated the King, unhappily eyeing the spreading stain of all that wasted ale, soaking into the last of the good tablecloths, "and one who was mad with greed. All he wanted was pazools, pazools, *pazools!*"

"The rotter!" said Mandricardo, sympathetically. "Cast a curse on the kingdom, what?" He was thinking of the trouble with a Wicked Wizard's curse they had had just recently over westaway in the two Pamphyllias, a curse in which he and his Amazonian lady-love had played a major role in the removing of, if you don't mind another dangling preposition, or whatever you call 'em.*

That particular Wicked Wizard, one Gorgonzola the Enchanter by name, had been a member in good standing of the Evil Magicians' and Wicked Enchanters' Guild, and it occurred to the Tartar knight to wonder if the local fellow might not belong to the same vile and infamous company . . .

"No; stole away me dotter," sighed King Akbar Akbad, wiping a tear from the corner of his eye on the tablecloth.

Callipygia started and swore a typically Amazonian oath, swearing by Hercules' toenails, or something. "Your *daughter?* I didn't know Your Majesty had a daughter?"

"Oh, yuss," said the King gloomily. "Had her for years, you know. Takes after her mother, she does. Perty gel; very perty. Bright brown eyes . . ."

Mandricardo cleared his throat and felt like rapping sternly on the table, to bring the conversation back to order.

"And what did the rogue *do* with the Princess, once he had carried her off, what?" he inquired sympathetically.

---

* The troubles in Pamphyllia are discussed in *Mandricardo*, chapters six through fifteen.

"Hid the poor gel away, nobody knows where," sighed King Akbad. "Place called 'the Topless Tower' . . . whatever *that* means."

"The Topless Tower," mused Callipygia, absently twirling one curl of her flowing locks about a finger.

"The Topless Tower," mused Mandricardo, fluffing out his mustaches fiercely, and smoothing one of the lion-skins he wore knotted about his breastplate to keep off the sun.

"The Topless Tower," mused Blundamore, knocking over the saltshaker.

"One more, ye say?" mumbled Braggadochio, wakening from a brief doze. "A-weel, only to restore the tissues, as ye'd say!"

It was after dinner when they were on their way upstairs to the bedrooms the King had assigned to his guests. He led them into a long shadowy-thronged gallery where oil portraits leered or frowned or simpered through the gloom.

"Sends me a portrait of the gel, he does, the swine, oncet a year, to show that she's in good health," sighed the King, hauling out an oil painting which he propped up at such an angle that it could catch the fading light.

It displayed a young girl of about sixteen or so, accoutered in the Eastern mode of dress, her features swathed but not concealed behind a filmy veil trimmed with luminous pearls. A silken turban crowned her small head, and snowy egret plumes floated therefrom, fastened by an aigret of topazes which matched her sparkling brown eyes.

She was entrancing. The King remarked that her name was Angelica— "Her blessed mother's notion, d'ye see; always had a head for history and such. Still and all, charmin' name . . ."

"Charming," repeated Sir Blundamore, who looked dazed . . . who looked, thought Mandricardo privately to himself, rather like an unsuspecting bull in the slaughterhouse who had just received the mallet between the eyes. "Whatever ails the chappie, what?" he muttered to himself.

"Holdin' her to ransom, d'ye see," grumbled the little King. "Me only chick nor child, and only heir to me kingdom . . . for half a million pazools."

"Half a *million*," repeated Sir Malaprop, dazedly. "Hell's bones! Felly'll be rich as a veritable Creosote, if you pay that!"

"Rich as a. . . ?" murmured Mandricardo, not quite getting it. Then he remembered Croesus, King of Lydia, reputed legendary for his wealth, and thought to himself with an indulgent chuckle, that you had to expect an occasional malapropism from someone who rejoiced in the fine old name of de Malaprop, after all.

He exchanged a knowing glance with Callipygia. They both giggled, and Malaprop, of course, never knew why.

Then, heaving a last fond sigh, King Akbad covered the portrait of his stolen daughter with tender hands, and led his guests on their way to the rooms assigned to them.

14

The Whereabouts of Angelica

Mandricardo had just completed his knightly task of cleansing the rust-flakes off his suit of armor, and burnishing and oiling the whole, and was relaxing with a nightcap of peppermint schnapps before the fire in his room and wishing (not for the first time) that he had brought along a squire on this adventure, if only to keep his armor furbished, when there came a timid knock on his door.

It was Sir Blundamore. The strapping youth wore a long flannel nightgown, which was too small for him and was stretched almost to the bursting point over his chest, which bulged with muscles, and his expression was at once sheepish and distracted and dreamy—an odd and virtually unique combination, from the experience of the Tartar.

"Oh, hullo," said Mandricardo.

"Hullo," said Blundamore. "I say, Mandro, may I come in for just a minute?"

The Tartar stepped aside and the young knight

139

came in, knocking over a side-table and breaking a lamp in the process. But that was only par for the course, for him. He wandered over to the mantlepiece, moodily declining Mandricardo's offer of a nightcap, and stood there fiddling with the small china ornaments, breaking only two or three.

"What's on your mind, old chap?" inquired the Tartar curiously. He had never before known Blundamore to be in such a strange mood of dreamy distraction.

"Oh, I don't know," murmured Blundamore. "I say, Mandro. . . ?"

"Yes, old chap?"

"That portrait the King showed us. Princess . . ."

". . . Angelica," offered Mandricardo helpfully.

"Angelica. Ah . . . handsome girl, didn't you think?"

"Quite," nodded Mandricardo. Then, remembering his position as an engaged man, and recalling that even the walls have ears, he added rather hastily, "Can't hold a candle to *Callipygia*, of course! But, still, yes . . . quite an attractive gel, if you like the Eastern sort. Almond-shaped eyes and olive skin and ruby lips, and all that sort of thing, you know."

"Yes," murmured Sir Blundamore, "all that sort of thing."

A silence of some duration ensued. Wearying at last of fiddling with, and breaking, the ornaments on the mantlepiece, the clumsy young knight flung himself into a chair drawn up before the fire, and managed to knock over and shatter a tall vase filled with peacock plumes. It is to be doubted if he even noticed having done so.

"Eyes like brown stars, wouldn't you say?"

" 'Brown stars,' " repeated Mandricardo, pursing his lips judiciously. "Well, yes, old chap, on the whole, I'd say that 'brown stars' about covered it."

"Lips like petals of the new-blown rose, perhaps?" suggested Blundamore.

" 'New-blown rose,' " murmured the Tartar, chewing on the end of one mustache. "Well, yes, now that you mention it . . ."

"Teeth like pearls?" said Blundamore dreamily.

At this suggestion, however, Mandricardo in all righteousness had to balk.

"Really couldn't say as to her *teeth*, old chap," he pointed out rather severely. "In the portrait, you know, her mouth was closed."

"Oh, yes, that's right, but, still . . . quite probably her teeth were like pearls," sighed Blundamore. "If her mouth had been open."

"Um," agreed Mandricardo, beginning to wonder if he was going to get any sleep at all that night, or sit up till dawn while sir Blundamore compared this and that and the other portion of the person of Princess Angelica of Sangaranga to a variety of precious or semiprecious minerals.

Before long, however, and heaving a deep-chested sigh, Sir Blundamore pulled himself up out of the embrace of the chair, tottered to the door, turned a wan and ghastly death's-head grin upon his host, and tottered out into the gloomy hall.

Mandricardo listened; shortly, there came the crash as the clumsy youth knocked over a table and smashed a mirror. The Tartar drew himself up to his full height, and shuddered.

"Young love!" he observed to himself, and went to bed.

*　　*　　*

All that next day they loitered around the royal palace of Sangaranga. Sir Malaprop, with many a self-important sniff, supervised a clutch or gaggle of stablehands, whom he had set to work polishing and waxing the Steed of Brass, until every flank and haunch and limb and whatever gleamed and glistened to his precise specifications.

Rather than have their presence cause a further strain to the palace kitchens, Callipygia suggested they go out of the capital and have a picnic on their own in the fields. Her bow brought down a brace of plump partridges and Sir Blundamore gathered a bonfire's-worth of dry wood, which Sir Malaprop set aflame with his Ever-Burning Coal (a handy item to have along on one's travels, what, as Mandricardo thought to himself).

They cooked and ate their own meal under the lazy shade of nodding trees. It was not, they had discovered, that the Sangarangians could not shoot down gamebirds with their bows and arrows in order to supplement their miserable diet, but that every gamebird they brought down they sold to foreign traders, mostly just across the border in the kingdom of Nexdoria, the funds from which transactions going toward the paying-off of the Wicked Wizard's ransom for Princess Angelica.

"I say, you chaps," said Mandricardo determinedly, after they had finished their lunch, "we shall have to do something about this Angelica business, what?"

"Raw*ther*, ker-hem," declared Sir Malaprop, who had just settled back against a quince tree for a nap, but who now roused himself (like an old warhorse at the sound of distant bugles) when he scented the whiff of knightly quests and chivalric endeavors in the tone of the Tartar's voice.*

"I mean to say, what? Can't have Wicked Wizards slitherin' about botherin' decent, law-abidin' citizens, can we now, what?"

"Certainly *not*," declared Sir Malaprop, nodding in firm agreement with the sentiments Mandricardo had just expressed.

"I mean, after all, Topless Towers and all that that sort of thing!" scoffed the Tartar knight. "Nice little country here, you know. Probably quite a pleasant place to visit, back when they had both cities and could lay a decent table, what?"

"Hear, hear!" said Malaprop, becoming drowsy again.

"Our knightly honor, you know," Mandricardo reminded them. "Chivalric oath, what? Damsels in distress . . . all that sort of thing, eh, what?"

Sir Blundamore uttered *a hollow moan* and rolled his eyes in his head, cracking his knuckles so loudly that Malaprop jumped, hak-kaffed, and glared about him suspiciously, as if wondering if some malicious child had not fired off a firecracker in the immediate vicinity, just to awaken him from his nap. As no such child was in evidence, the elderly little knight settled back to pick up the fallen threads of his snooze.

One did not have to be telepathic to understand the cause and nature of Blundamore's distress. The muscle-bound young knight had hoped (it was perfectly obvious) to have the quest to rescue

---

*If, that is, you can possibly "scent" anything in someone's tone of voice, which you can't, but I seem to have written myself into a corner here, and will grandly ignore the whole bothersome matter, and step grandly out of this footnote and back into the mainstream of my narrative.

Princess Angelica from the Wicked Wizard all to himself. And now it seemed as if half a dozen other knights would be clumping and clattering along, accompanying him on the expedition and getting their own share of the glory.

Once they had returned to the palace, Mandricardo sought out King Akbad, whom he found in the back-garden helping the stableboy hoe the parsnips, and struck up a brief conversation.

"I say, what ho! Just wonderin', you know, when this blighter Alibeck carried off the Princess, what, did you announce a quest and all that sort of thing? Usually done in such matters, you know."

"Of course, me boy," puffed the stout little King, swabbing his dripping brow vigorously with a red bandana handkerchief. "Knights and princes from thirty kingdoms round came clusterin' to sign up. But dashed few could find the Topless Tower, you know, and of them, none could manage to climb the blasted thing and bring down me little Angelica . . ."

And here the sentimental monarch paused to dash away a tear from the corner of his left eye.

"Um," remarked Mandricardo, shrewdly. He munched upon the right mustache which adorned his lip, as if somehow thereby to acquire a thought.

"Any idee why they couldn't climb the blighter?" he asked—to which King Akbad shrugged.

"No idee. Fellers were so shamefaced at havin' failed the quest, they mostly rode off without talkin'. Not that *I* blame them," he added magnanimously.

At the conclusion of this unsatisfying interview, the Tartar knight rejoined his companions, who were lazing around the palace courtyard, looking bored and fretful. All of them, that is, but for, Sir

Braggadochio, who had imbibed a bit too freely, perhaps, from his little black jug, and was sleeping off the effects of his liberal potations under a baobab tree, or whatever it was. *Some*thing exotic and Eastern, surely.

Anyway, Mandricardo reported the results of his conversation with King Akbad to his friends. As might be expected, they were not exactly delighted.

"Hell's bones," grumbled Sir Malaprop. "How are we s'posed to rescue this pore gel if we don't even know where she *is*? Mean to say, drat it all, can't rescue a damsel in distress if you can't even *find* 'er!"

"Quite," admitted Mandricardo moodily.

Callipygia swore by Theseus' left earlobe, or something, and said plaintively: "I guess we could zoom about Sangaranga on the Magic Flying Carpet and sort of look things over from above,* but . . . how do we recognize a 'Topless Tower' when we see one? Are they—or *it*—truly topless? And what does that *mean*, anyway?"

"Quite, m'love," sighed Mandricardo, chewing on the end of one mustache. The problem of the Topless Tower seemed . . . well, I was about to say *insurmountable,* and then realized what I was saying! A "tough one," let me hastily remark.

Just then, Sir Braggadochio awoke from his soothing slumbers. A beetle, perhaps, or some other small crawly creature, had entered the tempting aperture of his lips, parted in a soft snore, and, finding the alcoholic haze interesting, had

---

* The Amazon girl did not exactly use the term "aerial reconnaissance," since it had not yet been invented, but that was the gist of her suggestion.

ventured within. This, it seems, had roused our
hero from his nap, spitting and gagging until they
slapped him on his back.

A brief and gluggy restorative from his black
jug, while he listened to a reprise of their discussion, produced a remarkable and quite unexpected
response, from a source seldom tapped.

"Ah, foosh, moddom! If that's all that's botherin'
ye, let ol' Braggy set yere mind at rest the noo! *I*
know where the Princess is, ye ken!"

15

This Way to the Captive Princess

They all looked at him in surprise as he upended his magic jug and restored the tissues for a time. Wiping his dripping mustaches on the back of his hand, and drawing his breath harshly, he at length returned to the topic.

"Aye, foosh, gude sors and moddom, if *that* be all that's a-botherin' you, old Braggy can set everything peerfectly a-richt the noo! Yon Princess is near to hand, ye ken, and all weel shortly be a-weel!"

"But how do you ... I mean ... what makes you think ... that is ..." mumbled Mandricardo confusedly. He was not all all accustomed to having the man with the bristly red walrus mustache contribute much of anything to their councils, except to fall off a chair frequently, and utter Caledonian snores from the depths of *a sodden slumber*.

Oddly enough, the only one of their number who was not electrified by Braggadochio's pronouncement that he knew the secret hiding place of Princess Angelica was the one young man who might very reasonably be expected to find the pronouncement most ... ah ... well ... um ... electrifying.

And that, of course, was Sir Blundamore. It did not require too much perception to, um, perceive that the muscle-bound young knight seemed rather smitten with the portrait of Princess Angelica, she of the brown eyes. At the moment of Braggy's dramatic, if offhand, announcement, Blundamore was crouched in the background, scribbling away from time to time on a bit of parchment. Between scribbles he wrinkled up his brow, as if in the processes of deepest thought, and chewed absently on the other end of the pen.

He was engaged in writing a sonnet to Angelica's eyes. It was, reports the *Chronicle Narrative*, Blundamore's first attempt at composing a sonnet, and he was completely stuck trying to find a rhyme for "amber."

". . . Famber, gamber, hamber," he was mumbling to himself, as Braggadochio launched into his tale, after briefly taking aboard a pint or two of liquid refreshment.

Braggadochio allowed as how, the night before, he had "pairhops" partaken "a wee bit liberally" of the potent brew contained in his bottomless black jug. He awoke, it seems, with a stomach full of butterflies and a head that rang like an anvil being beaten by a team of round-the-clock blacksmiths.

"Weel, 'twas a braw lovely mornin' the noo, followin' a braw bricht nicht," he continued reminiscently, "so, afore takin' aboard me breakfast, I felt the need of fresh air and joost a bit o' exercise the noo. So I saddled up me Rosie and the twa of us went canterin' off for a brisk mornin' ride, d'ye ken?"

They kenned, all except for Sir Blundamore, still deep in his sonnet. He was muttering under his breath at the moment, ". . . Jamber . . . kamber . . . mamber . . . namber . . ." and was paying no attention to Braggy's rambling exposition.

"Oh, deary me, what a theerst, what a gert, fierce theerst a bit o' hard ridin' in the mornin' does work up in a mon," sighed the Caledonian knight, uncorking his jug and upending it gluggily for a time, in memory of that hard early morning ride.

"Never mind that, old chap," urged Mandricardo irritably. "The Princess! What about the Princess?"

Recorking his jug against some future hour of need, the walrus-mustached one gave them a canny wink and laid one finger shrewdly against a nose whose burst capillaries glowed rubescently like the very rose.

". . . Quamber . . . ramber . . . samber . . . tamber . . ." muttered Sir Blundamore in the background, looking miserable. The strapping young knight was beginning to suspect that there *was* no rhyme for "amber."*

"Yes, by Zeus' left eyelid, what about *the Princess*?" cried Callipygia between gritted teeth. These maundering locutions of Braggadochio's sometimes got on the nerves of his audience, who were at the end of their tether, waiting for him to get to the point. If point indeed there was.

"I dinna ken why yere so fashed, me good sor and moddom," declared Sir Braggadochio rather aggrievedly. "But what I was about to explain was . . . that on me ride I joost hoppened to discover

---

*And he was quite right, too. Try it yourself, if you don't believe me. Then you can try and find one for "orange."

where this Alibeck rogue had hidden away the puir lost and stolen lassie—!"

". . . Xamber . . . yamber . . . zamber . . ." mumbled the distracted Sir Blundamore in the background. Then he stopped suddenly—not only because he had come to the end of the alphabet, which would, of course, have been an excellent reason in its own right, but also because the meaning and import of Braggadochio's story had suddenly penetrated his sonnet-busied brain.

"You're . . . *sure?* Kaff?" barked Sir Malaprop.

"Oh, beyond a doot, me gude sor! Beyond a doot!" repeated Braggadochio, and fell off the end of the step upon which he had been seated, splashing into a low fishpond.

His unexpected, uninvited, and definitely unwelcome contact with the watery element, of which he was distinctly *un*fond, left Sir Braggadochio so shaken that it took them some little time to repair his composure. In this respect, frequent reliance upon the liquid contents of the little black jug proved salutary.

At length they donned their armor and took up their weaponry, stuffed into their saddlebags some lunch the Castle Cook whipped up for them, mounted their steeds and rode off in the direction indicated by the man with the walrus mustache. Indeed, now thoroughly dried but still from time to time shuddering at the memory of his narrow escape from a watery doom, the Caledonian knight led the way. True, he tended to sway a bit in the saddle, listing, I would say, on the whole, to port . . . and, also true, from time to time a tune escaped him which sounded suspiciously like that familiar old favorite, *"Scots wha hae wi' Wallace*

bled" . . . but still, as far as Mandricardo or
Callipygia could discern, Braggy seemed to know
where he was going, and was headed there with
all alacrity and dispatch.

They rode out of town and took a dusty path
which led through rising country and scrubby
woods toward dark lowering hills. These formed,
they had been given to understand, part of the
border between the kingdom of Sangaranga and
its neighbor, the kingdom of Nexdoria.

The Brazen Steed clattered and whirred and
clanked along, its smooth and stately stride eating
up the miles. Bayardetto and Blondel, by now
inured to their mechanical and lifeless (yet somehow magically animate) colleague, followed in its
dust. Sir Malaprop and Sir Blundamore, whom,
you will recall, had lost his white charger when the
two-headed Ogre selected him for the cookpot,
which was even before we met him in that iron-
barred cage—let me start this sentence over, as it
is becoming just a trifle too convoluted for even
me to follow: Sir Malaprop and Sir Blundamore
were both mounted astride the Horse of Brass.
Since the marvelous Horse was nearly as huge as
an elephant, there was enough room on its capacious back for three or four more, and not just the
two of them.

So that was the procession, with bony old Rosie
ambling along in her arthritic way in the lead,
with Braggadochio swaying in the saddle, puffing
away on his briar, mumbling his song under his
breath, and swinging his jug in time to the rhythm.
Quite a procession, as the various scrawny and
starving peasants, tinkers, farmers and gypsies along
the way, who stopped to marvel at the sight, would
attest.

*   *   *

The hills closed around them; they mounted a
steep and narrow pass whose walls, fortunately,
were *just* wide enough to afford passage for the
Steed of Brass.

"Do you think he knows where he's going?"
Callipygia asked Mandricardo after a time.

The Tartar knight chewed thoughtfully on the
ends of his mustaches.

"Dash it all, m'love, feller *seems* to know what he
talkin' about!" he grumbled. "Worth a try, anyway! If nothin' comes of it, well, dash it all, at
least, with any luck, you can bring down a brace of
pheasants or whatever—wild boar would be nice,
for a change, *dashed* nice!" he added, wistfully—
"for our supper, unless you care to try potluck
back at the castle again."

They chuckled over the thought. The Castle
Cook, they had learned through the friendly boot-
boy, had gone into nervous collapse upon learning that the five of them were *still* the guests of
King Akbad.

Oh, Sangaranga was *poor*, surely enough!

Braggadochio led them, at length, to the mouth
of a narrow pass in the hills—there was no imag-
ining whatever had impelled the inebriated knight,
earlier that morning, to wander in this particular
direction while off on his morning canter astride
his bony old nag—and here it was that he drew up
the reins, struck a dramatic pose, and gestured
grandly.

That this gesticulation also caused him to fall
out of the saddle was an incidental matter. People
like Sir Braggadochio become accustomed to falling down rather frequently, and soon learn to
take such things in their stride.

Clambering unsteadily to his feet, and dusting himself off with an oily bit of rag, he continued imperturbably:

"And the noo, my gude friends, as I cairtainly promised ye, we can bring this whole sorra business to an end, whurra, and be after rescuin' the puirr lassie from a horrible fate (I have nae doot, nae doot at all!) and soon be on our ain way hame, and dommed be all sorcerers and suchlike feelthy heathen!"

His second grandiloquent gesture—which this time was just a shade *less* grandiloquent—drew their attentions to a painted sign which was nailed to a bit of wood.

The sign pointed directly down the pass.

There was an inscription painted on the sign.

It read:

THIS WAY TO THE CAPTIVE PRINCESS.

BOOK FOUR

The Topless Tower

16

The Barbed Barrier

The travelers looked at the sign in stony silence, then stared at each other.

Mandricardo turned purple, chewed furiously on the ends of his mustaches and looked rather as if he might explode at any moment.

As for Callipygia, the Amazonian princess pressed her lips together, eyes sparkling, and seemd to be trying not to burst into hysterical peals of laughter.

Sir Blundamore merely tripped over a rock and fell down with a musical crash of his armor—which was not at all unusual for him.

Of them all, it happened to be Sir Malaprop who more or less put into words what each of them was thinking.

The elderly knight polished his eyeglasses vigorously, gave the roadsign another indignant glare, then muttered: "Hell's bones! Devil of a way to hide somebody you've kidnapped, what? I mean—putting up signs alongside the road! Demmed cheek, I call it!"

Callipygia nudged Blondel with her knees, and

the red mare moved forward and entered the
mouth of the pass. It proved not as narrow as it
looked; in fact, as far as Callipygia could judge
with the naked eye, even the Horse of Brass could
negotiate the narrow way. She rode back to where
the others still stood.

"Well?" demanded the Amazon girl crisply.
"We've come this far, we might as well keep going.
If Princess Angelica is anywheres about, well, here
we are to rescue her! Shall we, then?"

"Let's," nodded Mandricardo, and, once they
had gotten Sir Braggadochio back in the saddle,
and once Sir Blundamore had clambered back up
on top of the Brazen Steed, they entered the pass
and pressed on, eager to discover what mysteries
and perils it might hold for them.

Beyond the circle of the hills they found a medium-
smallish valley, but unfortunately another barrier
presented itself, and one far more imposing than
merely a bunch of hills.

To put it briefly, a solid wall of thorns rose in
their path. The thorny boughs, armed with wicked-
looking barbs up to four or even five inches in
length, were so tough and so thickly interwoven,
that they seemed nigh impenetrable. Also, the barrier rose to a height of about a dozen feet.

To say that the adventurers found this dispirit-
ing is to put it mildly. They were, in fact, dismayed.

"Bally thorns, what?" grumbled Mandricardo to
his lady-love. "You'd think this Princess Whatzer-
name was another dashed Madame La Belle a
Bois Dormant, wouldn't you, what?"*

---

* Mandricardo here refers to a famous heroine of Terra Magican
history, whom you will more readily recognize as "the Sleeping
Beauty of the Wood."

Malaprop was running over the options available to the rescuers; they became fewer and fewer as he considered them in turn.

"Can't cut our way through the thorns, of course; any fool could see that," grumbled the little man, polishing his spectacles as if to wear them away to nothing. "Must go on for half a mile or more! Can't set a fire and burn our way through them either . . . too dashed damp in these woods for that! Hell's bones, pore gel's going to have to languish in bally Durance Vile for a bit longer, what?"

"Um," said Mandricardo, stubbornly.

Suddenly, Blundamore spoke up. The brawny youth, now that he had given up on the hopeless task of writing a sonnet to the amber eyes of Angelica, began to come into his own . . . as shall shortly be seen, not far up ahead.*

"The Horse of Brass!" he exclaimed—Blundamore, that is.

"What about it, kaff?" inquired Sir Malaprop, who, as the discoverer of the celebrated relic, had a proprietary interest in the creature. Or mechanism. Or whatever.

"Well, none of our living steeds could possibly force a passage through that wall of thorns, since they are flesh and blood," said Blundamore. "But the Brazen Steed could do it, and easily, because its hide is solid metal, and it can't feel the sting of the thorns!"

"Um," said Malaprop, pursing his lips judiciously.

"Not only that, but all of us could climb aboard,"

---

* You know—it struck me, quite suddenly—one of the interesting things about being an author is *knowing* what is coming up ahead. Odd that this never occurred to me before; but it never did.

continued Blundamore. "There's enough room atop
the Steed for every one of us, *and*, since the creature is at least twice the height of the tallest stallion *I* ever heard of, if we draw our knees up, the
Steed can carry us through the thorns unscathed.
I think I mean unscathed. Un*scratched*, anyway . . .
what do you think?"

"Um," said Malaprop again. "Ruin the polish,
those thorns would . . ."

"Oh, *bother* the polish, what!" cried Mandricado
excitedly. "Brass can be polished and repolished
until the cows come home . . . in fact, if this works,
and we rescue Princess Angelica and defeat the
Wicked Wizard Whatzisname—"

"Alibeck the Avaricious," Callipygia reminded
him. He shrugged the unnecessary information off
rather impatiently.

"*Bother* the dashed wizard! If this works, I'll
have the bally Steed plated in gold at me own
expense, what?"

At times, Mandricardo tended to get carried
away just a bit, from his own natural enthusiasm.
Still and all, he still had plenty of gold dinars in
his saddle bags, not to mention those pigeon's-
blood rubies Sir Kesrick had shared with him.

"Well, I, ah, um," said Sir Malaprop lamely.

They returned to the grassy plain beneath the
hills, where they unsaddled Bayardetto, Blondel
and Rosie and let them loose to *crop the dewy sward*,
and to do whatever else it is that horses do when
they are free and unobserved.

Then the adventurers mounted upon the back
of the Steed of Brass, with Sir Malaprop, of course,
as was only his natural right, at the helm, or the
reins, or the controls, or whatever the proper term

should be. But just then, Mandricardo excused himself and slid back off the back of the towering brass creature and returned to where they had hidden their gear and saddles and stuff, under a spreading bush.

He shortly returned, lugging under one arm a dusty and dilapidated bundle of worn and faded cloth which they, of course, recognized as the Magic Flying Carpet. This he tossed up to Callipygia and clambered aboard the Brazen Steed again.

"Too valuable to leave behind, what," he puffed, as he regained his seat. "Rogues and reivers about, no doubt. And, besides, never know just when a Magic Flying Carpet may come in handy on these adventures, what?"

"Quite," nodded Sir Blundamore.

"Let's get going," suggested Callipygia.

Sir Malaprop, of course—and it was only his natural right, as discoverer and present owner of the Steed of Brass—took his place at the reins, or controls, or whatever you wish to call them. With many a self-important little ker-haff and ker-hem he set the immense mechanical creature into action. The sparkling brass marvel assaulted the thorny barrier, and they watched as the crushing weight of its ponderous hooves of glinting brass broke down and crushed underfoot—or do I mean *underhoof?*—the thorny boughs, no matter how thick, how tough, or how springy.

Slowly, and then with gathering force, the Brazen Steed began to cleave through the thorns like a locomotive through a barrier of cardboard. The passengers drew their legs up and hugged their knees as the topmost thorny boughs lashed about as if striving to scratch them.

Erelong they were safely through the thick wall

of thornbushes and discovered themselves at the lip of a small and shallow vale whose cup dipped down through mazy streams and little dells and dingles and things, to the base of—

A tower!

"Oh, I say, dash it all!" breathed Sir Mandricardo delightedly. "Bally old Topless Tower itself, eh, what? Now, *this* is my sort of a quest, what?"

The others, while interested in the view, could not help looking just a bit skeptical. It was the Amazonian princess who pointed out one minor flaw in her Tartar lover's enthusiastic pronouncement.

"*Some* Topless Tower," she remarked sarcastically. "Looks about forty feet tall to me, and if that conical copper roof isn't a top, well, I've never seen one—!"

"Um," agreed Sir Mandricardo, stuffing one end of his mustache in his mouth and begin to chew upon it moodily, as was, for some reason, his wont.*

"But—this *must* be the Topless Tower, after all," cried Sir Blundamore, almost falling off the Steed of Brass in his excitement. "For look—that big window on the top story—it's the Princess Angelica!"

---

* I happen to have supported a mustache myself, off and on, for some years, and I must remark that *chewing* upon one seems to me the most insanitary of habits. Still and all, I'm not a Tartar, of course, and there may be something in that.

17

Why the Tower was Called "Topless"

They looked, and saw that Sir Blundamore was certainly right—it was, could only be, the kidnapped princess. There were those amber eyes that had so haunted Blundamore and had proved so impossible to rhyme; a filmy veil (after the Eastern manner) floated over the lower part of her face, but did little to conceal her ruby lips and pearly teeth. A huge silken turban was wrapped about her brows and the snowy plumes of egrets floated therefrom, pinned to the fabric with huge brooches of topaz.*

Spotting them far below her window, she waved a gauzy kerchief and called down to them.

"Yoo-hoo! Have you good people come to set me free?"

"What ho!" boomed Mandricardo in high good

---

* Since the Princess Angelica had been spirited away by the Wicked Wizard at the very beginning of his nefarious plot against Sangaranga, she still had gems while the remainder of her father's wealth, and all *his* jewels, had gone to pay the ransom.

humor, doffing his helm courteously. "Princess Angelica, I presume, what?"

"The very same, sir knight," she replied. "Then you *have* come to rescue me! Goody! It's been such a long time since I saw any knights or champions around here, I had begun to think everyone had forgotten about poor little me."

"Not at all, not at all," said Mandricardo grandly. "Pray permit me to introduce myself and company. I am hight Sir Mandricardo of Tartary, and this fair lady is hight Princess Callipygia of Amazonia," and he went on to explain what everybody else was hight, not forgotting Sir Blundamore, who, scarlet to the tips of his ears, essayed a deep bow and fell into a berry bush, which made Angelica laugh merrily.

Dismounting from the Horse of Brass, our heroes examined the so-called Topless Tower. It was Callipygia who discovered—by the simple expedient of walking all the way around the structure—that it had no door, or, at least, none that was clearly visible. Neither did it have any windows at all, until you got to the very top, right under the conical roof of green copper, where Angelica had her apartment.

"Do you suppose that's why nobody could get to the top and bring the girl down?" mused the Amazon.

"Mebbe so," said the Tartar. "Forty foot is forty foot, and even though that isn't exactly topless, what, it's a decent, a quite respectable height, for a tower . . ."

"Too tall for a ladder to reach the top, kaff!" added Sir Malaprop, polishing his spectacles.

"Precisely!" nodded Mandricardo. They stood in a row, fingering their jaws or whatever, frowning upon the problem. From the topmost window, Angelica from time to time, encouragingly fluttered her gauzy kerchief. Halfheartedly, they waved back at her, when they remembered to.

It was Blundamore who pointed out the most obvious solution to their problem. He had discovered a stout and ancient ivy vine which clung stubbornly to the ancient stone of the tower, and whose topmost boughs all but brushed the bottom sill of Angelica's window. Mandricardo looked dubious.

"Don't have a very good head for heights, meself," the Tartar knight admitted.

"Well, *I* do!" maintained the blond young knight in vigorous tones. "And, besides, this is my dashed quest, anyway! If I rescue the Princess, I win her hand in marriage . . . and you've already got yourself a fiancée."

"That he surely does," said Callipygia flatly. Mandricardo turned pink, just a little, under his natural swarthiness.

"Not tryin' to horn in on yer quest at all, old chap!" he protested. "Of course—climb to the window and fetch down the pore gel, and we'll all be back to the castle in time for a late lunch."

"Best take off your armor and weapons first," advised the Amazon princess. "Make you lighter, you know. Don't want you to take a tumble—especially not while carrying down Angelica!"

Blundamore promptly removed every bit of his armor, making a neat pile of it at the foot of the ivy, and then, with a friendly hail to the Princess watching coyly from above—something more or less in the mood of "Here I come, ready or not!" —the muscular youth sprang up, clutched the sturdy ivy bough, swung up further, found convenient footholds, and began to climb.

Now forty feet is forty feet, and I wouldn't care to have attempted the feat myself, not particularly . . . however, it was not beyond the bounds of credibility that such as Blundamore* could without great difficulty have scaled the tower to its top and then clambered down again, with the Princess Angelica clinging to his back.

But it was then that the adventurers discovered exactly why the structure was called *the Topless Tower*. . . .

Sir Blundamore had gotten nearly to the top—he was about seven or eight or nine feet below the window sill—when the Uncanny began to occur.

The topmost part of the Tower began to *stretch* like the neck of an ostrich. Or like a piece of rubber. Or like whatever you care to mention that stretches—let us not quibble.

And while Blundamore watched helplessly, Angelica, brown eyes and all, was carried hopelessly beyond his reach—for the ivy, you will understand, did *not* stretch, and grew no higher than it had been all along. . .

Which was not high enough.

While Blundamore rested against a tree in the shade, puffing and blowing and fanning himself, they discussed the problem, which had suddenly become a lot more serious than at first they had thought it would . . . ah . . . become.

---

* And you mustn't forget what I said earlier about him being so strong. "Even his muscles had muscles" is one phrase that particularly springs to mind.

Angelica had written a note (on scented paper, and in a *flawless Spencerian hand,* as befits one of the blood royal), the which she had wrapped around a small brass snuffbox, which she tossed out of her window. It fell, unfortunately, on Braggadochio's head. That worthy, taking an early afternoon's siesta, awoke suddenly, believing himself the target of a shower of meteorites—and it took some persuading before they managed to relieve his trepidations. It read as follows.

Dear Sir Mandricardo of Tartary, and All, especially that very brave young man who tried to climb up the ivy to rescue me.

The Topless Tower stretches and stretches, so that the upper floor (where I have my little pied-à-terre) always stays out of reach of anyone trying to climb up to reach me. This is the cunning plan of Alibeck, that villain!

I know of no way that you could circumvent his magical spell . . . but I certainly wish you well, especially that handsome young man who tried to climb the ivy and rescue me. What was his name again?

Very best wishes to you all, and have a nice day!
                                        Angelica F.

Our heroes thereupon retired to the shade of the Steed of Brass for a conference. As none of them had any particular idea to offer, this conference proved so brief that they called it off in favor of lunch. The Castle Cook had packed them a meager repast, which Callipygia eyed with extreme disfavor. There were watercress sandwiches and a few overripe apples, somewhat wrinkled and sour by now, and a rind or two of goat's-cheese, and a covered pot of gruel or mush or something whose principal ingredient seemed to be stewed lentils.

As Callipygia was a hearty girl with a thriving appetite, the meal did little to satisfy her inner needs. "If I ever intend to go on a diet," the Amazon princess grumbled to herself, "This visit to Sangaranga affords me the perfect opportunity . . ."

In fact, she reflected, a visitor to Sangaranga was dieting whether or not he or she really wished to.

For the next hour or two, the adventurers discussed this or that solution to their problem, but without finding a solution thereto. All the while, Angelica kept tossing down from above encouraging little notes written in that flawless and flowing hand of hers upon her crested note-paper.

These bore messages like—

> *Be not discouraged, do not fear—*
> *Stick with it, and you'll persevere!*

And—

> *If at the first you try and fail,*
> *Stay firm of purpose, do not weep;*
> *Just keep it up and you'll prevail,*
> *Thus many breezes make a gale*
> *And lambs grow into great big fat sheep.*

And other helpful homilies of encouragement doubtless learned by the Princess at the rheumatic knee of her old nurse when she was a child.*

"A trifle wobbly in the scansion department," said Sir Blundamore critically of this last note, "but you have to agree with the sentiment."

There was even one note which read—

---

*When *Angelica* was a child, I mean. Not her nurse.

A stitch in time saves plenty more,

but it was obvious by that time that the Princess
had run out of applicable adages, and was grasp-
ing at straws. Shortly thereafter the rain of messages from above came to a halt, and I have no
doubt that the reason for this was that Angelica
was in the habit of taking a little nap or brief siesta
after luncheon, rescuing knights or no rescuing
knights.

Sir Braggadochio thereupon retired to the shade
of a convenient mulberry bush and consulted the
bottom of his magic black jug for inspiration, falling into a doze himself. Blundamore, depressed
by his failure to climb the enchanted tower, wandered about scowling and kicking rocks and occasionally falling over one in the process. Sir Malaprop was comfortably seated on the emerald sward
with his back propped up against one of the fore-
legs of the Brazen Steed; he was smoking his
after-lunch cigar and humming a little tune to
himself and daydreaming about the Galumphing
Beast, no doubt.

As for Mandricardo and Callipygia, they sat a
little ways apart, discussing the situation in low
tones so as not to disturb their companions in
adventure.

Just another lazy afternoon in sunny Sangaranga,
I suppose you could call it.

Meanwhile, what of the author of all their troubles? I refer to the avaricious Alibeck, the Wicked
Wizard who happens to be the villain of our story,
but who has yet to make his first appearance on
stage (as it were) in this narrative.

As it chanced, he was watching this very scene at

this very moment through his magic crystal, and was not in the slightest degree alarmed or trepidatious at the arrival of so many stalwart champions of law and justice at the foot of the magical edifice in which he had imprisoned the poor Princess. The reason for this was that he knew they could not succeed in getting the Princess down from her enchanted eyrie, so what did it matter if they were half-a-dozen or a half-a-hundred in number?

Stifling a slight yawn behind a polite palm, he switched off the magic crystal—oh, *you* know what I mean!—and went to have his own lunch.

We shall see more of him just a little later.

18

A Stitch in Time

Now, this Alibeck commonly resided in a cavern in the mountains directly to the east of the kingdom of Sangaranga. It was a cave whose rugged walls were hewn of sparkling blue mineral, the interior softly illuminated by magic lights which drifted to and fro like luminous moths.

In the center of the rocky floor was a pool or spring, filled to the brim with cold, pure, crystal-clear water which bubbled up from the bottom of the world. At one end of the pool there grew the most peculiar tree you have ever seen or heard of. Its leaves were shavings of thin green jade which tinkled like wind-chimes to the impulse of the captive little breeze which circulated the air in Alibeck's cavern, and the bark and stems and branches of this tree were of a mixture of silver and gold—an alloy called electrum.

The fact that Alibeck's enchanted tree was fashioned entirely of metal and mineral did not, however, restrain it from bearing fruit—and fruit is precisely the *mot juste*. For Alibeck had his theories

on what was healthy to eat and what was un-
healthy to eat, as he had theories on just about
everything else under the sun, and according to his
theories a man should only drink pure water and
eat nothing but fruit.

Thus the gold-and-silver branches of the magic
tree bore living fruit ... apples, grapes, pome-
granates, bananas, peaches, apricots, pineapples,
plums and pears. Here in the Lands We Know, we
would probably call Alibeck the Avaricious a vegetarian,* and his odd diet may have been accountable for his short temper and mean and vicious
character, for I would say that a man who takes a
drop or two of wine or good brown ale once in a
while tends to be better-humored than one who
drinks only cold water from a mountain spring,
and is on the whole friendlier and more neigh-
borly if he also takes aboard a bit of roast beef or
fried chicken or baked ham, than one who does
not.

His all-fruit diet also was responsible for his
appearance, for Alibeck was *extremely thin*. His legs
were like two dry sticks, and so were his arms,
and, as he was quite tall (for a Wicked Wizard),
you could not help noticing this about him.

At the moment, he was perched atop a tall stool
propped in front of a high lectern. Upon this
lectern was a huge ledger book in which the Wicked
Wizard was writing with a quill pen fashioned from
the plume of some purple bird. What he was doing
was entering the most recent installment of the
ransom money he was wringing from the poor,
hungry, poverty-stricken Sangarangians, which sum

---

* Well, he was actually a *fruitatarian*, but there doesn't seem to be
any such word, at least not in my dictionary.

he added to the total thus far extorted. He was grinning hugely, for the bigger the total became, the happier it made his cruel and greedy heart, and this toothy leer, when considered in conjunction with his great bony beak of a nose, made him very much resemble a gloating vulture.

His skinny frame was wrapped in an old, much-patched, threadbare bathrobe of some cheap snuff-colored cloth, and he wore an ancient, dilapidated pair of carpet slippers on his bony feet.

Like all misers, it was purely the accumulating of money, of wealth, which delighted him—not the *spending* of it. And so he commonly wore his clothes until they were literally falling to rags and pieces, rather than buy new ones.

There was no sound in the sparkling blue cavern, save for the scratching of Alibeck's quill pen on the pages of the ledger book and the gurgling of water in the pool, as it came bubbling up from far below.

Then suddenly there sounded the shrill clangor of an unseen gong.

Alibeck blenched, gasped, and dropped his pen. Then, giving utterance to a shriek of insane fury, he snatched up his magic wand, and promptly vanished from view.

For his favorite enchantment had just been . . . *broken!*

The afternoon was sunny and hot, and by this time all of our little band of heroes were napping in the shade, except for Sir Blundamore. The muscular young knight was seated—rather uncomfortably, as a matter of fact—on a boulder. He was scowling in deep thought, gnawing on his bottom lip, and much too annoyed at his failure to rescue Princess Angelica by the simple expedient of climb-

ing the ivy and carrying her down from the top of
the Topless Tower, to seek respite from the heat
of the summary day with a soothing little siesta in
the shade of the Steed of Brass.

From time to time, the lovelorn young man
would draw a packet of crested and scented note
paper from beneath his armor, where he wore
this against his heart. These were the various cheerful and encouraging homilies that Angelica had
tossed down to her champions a bit earlier. As
they had come from her very lilylike hands, they
were precious to Blundamore. He read them over
and over, smiling fondly and taking heart from
their little messages.

All of them, that is, save for the one which
read—

A stitch in time saves plenty more,

which, of course, really had nothing at all to do
with their present problem of rescuing the Princess from her captivity.

Or . . . *did* it?*

He had just read this last little note for the
hundred-and-thirty-second time, and was folding
it and putting it back with the others, pressed
against his heart and just under his cuirass, when,
as it happened, his wandering gaze fell on the
worn and faded roll of fabric Mandricardo had
fetched along with them, as it was much too valuable to leave behind for rogues, reivers and

---

* Personally, I am of the opinion that the Fairy Whitethorn had a
hand in the penning of that particular note, but the *Chronicle
Narrative* does not say, and, since the Fairy Whitethorn has not as
yet come into our story, I am being premature.

robbers—if there were still any left in Sangaranga, where there was hardly anything remaining which was worth roguing, reiving and robbing.

He noticed absently that the worn old Carpet (for we are talking anout the Magic Flying Carpet, you will understand) had a long rent in the part of it which was facing him.

The tear looked dangerous to him. "Could use a bit of mending, I suppose," mused Blundamore. "A few stout stitches should do the trick, I fancy. Otherwise, someday someone will be going up in the Carpet—I mean, *on* the Carpet—and just might fall through. Or flying *down*, as the case may be . . ."

And at that moment the musclebound youth came suddenly to his feet with a yell, leaping up with as much alacrity as you or I would doubtless display, had we suddenly and unexpectedly happened to sit down on a bristly cactus.

His loud yell brought the rest of the little party of adventurers wie awake on the instant, and scrambling to their feet in alarm.*

"Have at you—varlets! Rogues!" roared Sir Mandricardo, snatching up his trusty broadsword and glaring around him, wild-eyed. He was obviously under the impression that a herd of Ogres or *something even worse* had crept upon them unobserved, while they were enjoying their little nap in the cool shade.

But, of course, there were no Ogres to be seen.

---

* All, that is, except for Braggadochio, who had turned up his nose in fastidious contempt at the scanty potluck the Castle Cook had scraped up to serve as their lunch. The knight had taken aboard a liquid lunch, as was rather often his wont, and thus snored blissfully through most of what was shortly to ensue.

They were alone in the thorn-bordered little vale where the Topless Tower stood.

"Hell's bones, what is it now, ker-haff?" snapped Sir Malaprop testily, clambering laboriously to his feet. The stout little old knight dearly loved his nap and hated to be so rudely awakened. Peering about, he could see nothing sufficiently untoward to have occasioned Blundamore's cry of alarm.

Callipygia, who had strung her bow and nocked an arrow with lightning-swift motions, now un-strung the weapon and fixed Sir Blundamore with a look that could probably fry an egg at twenty paces.

"I certainly hope you have a good explanation for yelling in my ear like that, you great clumsy oaf," she said in ominous tones. "I was enjoying the most delightful dream, just when you yelled loudly enough to rouse the dead—"

The muscle-bound blond youth turned pink to the tips of his ears and looked sheepish. He cleared his throat.

"Oh, I say! Sorry to have awakened you so sud-denly, and all that sort of thing," he said. But he did not look in the least perturbed . . . in fact, his face was wreathed with the hugest grin you have ever seen or imagined.

He looked like a man with a secret.

"Oh, say nothing of it, old chap," yawned Mandricardo, as he replaced his broadsword in its scabbard (there being no Ogres in sight). "Sup-pose it's time we were waking up, anyway . . . can't slumber the afternoon away, you know—not when there are damsels in distress to be rescued from Durance Vile!"

As if on cue, Princess Angelica waved her ker-chief from the tower window and called down

"Yoo-hoo!" just to let them know that she had awakened from her postprandial nap, as well as had the rest of them.

They waved and yoo-hooed back politely; then the Amazonian princess returned her attentions to Sir Blundamore.

"Well?" she demanded crossly. "We are waiting for an explanation, you know. You still haven't explained why you woke us up with such an ear-splitting shout."

"Quite right, quite right," puffed Sir Malaprop, giving the young knight a severe glance over the tops of his little spectacles. "Hell's bones, lad—I thought it was the dear beast who had suddenly hove into view!"

"Nothing like that, I'm afraid," admitted Blunamore. Then he turned to the tall Tartar, who also stood waiting for some sort of an explanation for Blundamore's curious behavior.

"I say, Mandro—do you mind if I borrow the Magic Flying Carpet for a few minutes? An idea just popped into my head a few moments back, and I would very much like to give it a try . . ."

"Why, certainly, old chap," said the Tartar in affable tones. "But if you're thinking that, just because the Carpet can ascend to the sky much more swiftly, what, than you can climb the ivy, you're very likely to catch the Tower by surprise, I'll wager that you're mistaken . . ."

Blundamore shook his blond head.

"No, it isn't that—although that's worth a try, too," he said.

"Well, go ahead then, m'boy," gestured Mandricardo. "Help yourself to the Carpet, although I'm dashed if I can see another way it can be of any use to us in our present predicament."

Blundamore murmured his thanks, and clambered up the side of the Horse of Brass to take down the motheaten and threadbare roll of Carpet.

That last, and seemingly pointless, homily which the Princess of Sangaranga had earlier tossed down to the encouragement of her gallant rescuers had given Sir Blundamore an idea.

And he thought he knew exactly how to rescue Angelica!

19

Sir Blundamore to the Rescue

Mandricardo and Callipygia lent Sir Blundamore a hand, and between them they unrolled the Carpet and spread it out neatly on the grass. With that uncanny sense which it seems Flying Carpets possess, the dilapidated bit of woven cloth somehow realized that on this trip it would have only one or two passengers, and not the lot of them, horses and all. So it reduced its dimensions to more suitable proportions.

Then the young knight seated himself in the center and instructed the Carpet to fly. He had decided to try first the notion which the Tartar knight had mentioned, before attempting his own idea. So, at his bidding, the Magic Flying Carpet soared upward with breathtaking speed, circling 'round and 'round the Topless Tower and ascending toward the sky very rapidly ... *very* rapidly indeed.

But this accomplished exactly nothing, as the tall Tartar had predicted. The enchanted struc-

ture merely stretched its queerly elastic stone a
little bit faster than the Carpet could ascend, and
in no time at all its upper works were lost in the
clouds above.

"Told him so," muttered Mandricardo under
his breath. But he would dearly have loved to be
proven wrong.

Giving up that particular method, Blundamore
ordered the Carpet to descend, which it did;
promptly, the Topless Tower reduced its own
height until it had again achieved its customary
altitude, which, as I may have remarked earlier,
was about forty feet from the ground.

Sir Malaprop, who had been observing with interest these goings-on, now shaded his eyes against
the late-afternoon sun. "What's the lad doin' now?"
he inquired.

"Dashed if I know," admitted Mandricardo.
"Seems to be flyin' off into the east for some
reason . . ."

"Now he's going right straight up in the air,"
remarked Callipygia in tones of mystification. "But
he's nowhere near the Tower . . . what on earth
does he think he's up to?"

When the blond young knight had risen to the
level of the clouds—the Tower remaining at its
usual height of forty feet or so, since the Magic
Flying Carpet was nowhere near enough to afford
it any sort of threat—he flew the Carpet directly
over the Tower.

Then he began to rapidly descend.

The Topless Tower began to shiver and quiver
like a live thing caught in a trap.

It jerked a little from left to right, but there was
no way the enchanted structure could escape from
under the rapidly descending Carpet.

It began to reduce its height!

As Mandricardo, Callipygia and Sir Malaprop watched enthralled, the Tower shrank to thirty-five feet in height . . . then thirty . . . twenty-five . . . twenty . . .

"Deuced clever, that young chap!" breathed the stalwart Tartar, overcome with admiration for the quick wits of Sir Blundamore. Chivalrous to the very core of his being (whatever that means), Mandricardo was always ready to give credit where credit was due.

And right now credit was due Sir Blundamore.

"Hell's bones," remarked Sir Malaprop, "never would have thought of it, meself. Deuced clever of the young felly, as you say!"

By now the top of the Topless Tower was hardly more than ten feet off the ground, and Mandricardo and his Amazonian lady-love sprinted forward to assist the Princess Angelica to climb over the sill of her window and down onto the ground.

The very moment her dainty slipper touched the greensward, the enchantment was broken.

There was a flash of sour greenish light which dazzled their eyes momentarily. Then their nostrils were assaulted by a ghastly and quite inescribable stench—

And the Tower vanished like a pricked soap bubble. There no longer remained so much as a wrack of it behind, to show that the magical edifice had ever stood upon this spot—except for a hole in the ground where the foundations of the Topless Tower had been.

They clustered about the slim form of the Princess Angelica, who swayed gracefully, momentarily overcome by the emotions only natural to one who has returned to the surface of the earth after having been for so long imprisoned in the sky.

Mandricardo helped her to seat herself in Braggadochio's folding lawn chair, while Callipygia fanned the Princess with her helm and Sir Malaprop hastened to unstopper and put to her ruby lips a silver flask of potent cordial he always wore upon his person to recruit his vigor when overcome by fatigue, or whatever.

"A thousand, thousand thanks to my gallant and resourceful rescuers!" Angelica said sweetly, having recovered herself. "But where is the brave and handsome young chevalier who succeeded where so many others before him failed in breaking the vile enchantment of the villainous Alibeck?"

They turned to look about, finding that by now the Magic Flying Carpet had settled to earth as gently and as silently as a fluttering autumn leaf. And there stood Blundamore, the hero of the hour, blushing a furious crimson.

"My hero!" she sighed rapturously, eyelashes fluttering.

And Blundamore blushed an even deeper crimson. If possible.

"Hell's bones," remarked Sir Malaprop from some little ways away. "Do come and look at what I've found!" They turned to discover him standing on the edge of the hole where the foundations of the Topless Tower had been. The bald and elderly little knight was staring into the cavity.

As well he might! When the others came over to join him where he stood, they saw to their amazement that the hole (which was much bigger than at first it had seemed) was filled almost to the brim with . . . *treasure*.

"I *say*," marveled Mandricardo, thunderstruck.

"Bally riches of Creosote, what, what?" muttered Malaprop proudly.

"The riches of poor, starved Sangaranga, more than likely," Callipygia pointed out. And, of course, as it turned out, she was entirely correct. And where better should the avaricious Alibeck have concealed the ransom of the Princess than beneath the very Tower in which he had imprisoned her? A certain poetic justice in that, you will have to admit . . .

There were coins aplenty, copper, bronze, silver and gold; and bars and wedges and ingots of precious metals; and wagonloads of rings, brooches, necklaces, tiaras, pins, armlets, chains and other ornaments and baubles. And there were sacks of rubies, chests of sapphires, bags of emeralds, caskets of diamonds, boxes of topazes and amethysts and garnets and other gems. To say nothing of all the jade and amber and ivory and ambergris and myrrh and . . . but I'm sure you get the idea.

It was the entire wealth of a kingdom.

"Dash it all, how on earth are we supposed to get it all back to the city?" complained Mandricardo. "We can't just leave the treasure trove laying out in the open like this for, well, *anybody* to come along and claim for his own!"

"A couple of us will have to stay behind to guard the trove, while the rest of us carry the glad word back to the King," suggested the Amazon girl.

They agreed that this seemed to be the best

idea. Sir Malaprop cleared his throat self-importantly.

"Hem! Braggy and I will take charge here," he decided. "We would have—kaff!—some difficulty in rousing the poor chap from his snooze anyway, considering all of his favorite beverage the felly consumed in lieu of lunch. I suspect," he said to Mandricardo, "that you will need to borry the Horse of Brass to get back through all those thornbushes. Blighters seem to be enchanted, too, just like the bally Tower—notice all the path the Steed trampled down in getting us here have by now grown back just the way they were before?"

And he was quite right, too, although none of them had noticed the fact before he pointed it out. The thorny barrier was every bit as thick and tall in the pass as it had originally been.

They packed up their gear and stored it back aboard the Steed of Brass,* including Braggy's folding lawn chair and the picnic basket the Castle Cook had packed for them. Then they rolled up the Magic Flying Carpet and stowed it away within the hollow haunches of the Steed.

Then they were ready to board the mechanical marvel for the trip back to the capital.

Blundamore—whose manners were certainly princely, even if he did rather tend to trip over things and fall down a lot—politely offered Angelica his arm.

"Permit me, Princess, to assist you to ascend,"

---

* I notice that I forgot to mention earlier that the rear haunches of this marvelous mode of transportation were hollow and opened, like the trunk of an automobile, to disclose storage space. I can't be expected to remember *everything*, you know.

he offered. She rewarded him with a demure smile that could have melted a snowbank.

"*So* gallant!" the Princess whispered, fluttering those long eyelashes again. The love-stricken young knight crimsoned again, but helped her up to the high saddle without accident. Then he clambered up after her, and assumed a position just behind Callipygia and Mandricardo, who had already mounted and were ready to depart, with the Tartar knight at the controls of the Steed.

"We'll be back as soon as we can, old boy," Mandricardo called down to Sir Malaprop, "so you just hold the fort here."

"To be sure, to be sure," puffed Sir Malaprop. "But *do* try to get back before nightfall, won't you, me boy? I've no particular wish to spend half the night guardin' a hole full of treasure in the dark and cold and damp . . ."

"Tut, we'll do our best, old chap," said Mandricardo reassuringly. "And the sooner we depart, the quicker we'll be able to return in order to relieve you of your sentry-go, what? So we're off—"

As it happened, however, they did not depart as swiftly as they had intended.

For there came what might be termed an untimely interruption in their plans—

The little clearing between the walls of thorny bushes was dim with the lengthening shadows of late afternoon (or early twilight, if you prefer).

These gloomy shadows were lit, quite suddenly, by a blinding flash of bilious light the precise color of sour green apples. The swift burst of illumination was accompanied by a stench of such nostril-withering horrendousness that it would have made a vulture gag.*

"*No*body is going *no*where," said a nasty, sneering voice from behind their backs. His grammar was atrocious; but, then, why should a Wicked Wizard worry about his grammar?

For of course it was the villain of our tale—Alibeck the Avaricious.

---

* You know, it never occurred to me before, but a feat of evil magic should very likely be accompanied by a bad smell, and such.

20

The Undoing of Alibeck

Before them there had melted into being the tall, gaunt figure of the Wicked Wizard, his skinny frame wrapped in that patched old bathrobe, dilapidated carpet slippers on his bony feet, clutching his magic wand in clawlike fingers. This was a rod of thin black wood with serpents twined around it, like a caduceus ... except that in this case, the serpents were live and wriggling.

Oh, and I forgot to mention—when I described him back in Chapter Eighteen—that he wore an old bath towel wrapped about his knobby, bald brows in lieu of the usual turban. The reason for this, quite simply, was that Alibeck had worn out his last turban, and was much too cheap to go out and buy some new ones.

"I say, m'dear," Sir Mandricardo murmured in confidential tones to Princess Angelica, "but this wouldn't be that Wicked Wizard of yours, would it, what?"

The Princess shuddered, and rested one hand on his brawny arm, swaying as if about to swoon.

"Not *mine*, sir knight, not *mine!*" she protested, "but it *is* none other than he, the dastardly villain!"

Both Sir Blundamore and the Tartar knight exchanged stern glances, and drew their trusty blades—but Alibeck gestured with his wand (hissing vipers and all), and they froze motionless from the waist down, as unable to take a step forward as if their lower limbs had been struck to stone by the glance of a passing Basilisk, or something like.

"I say, that's not cricket, old boy," said Mandricardo, rather aggrievedly. "Paralyzing a fella's feet . . . simply isn't done in the best of circles, you know!"

The Wicked Wizard sneered at him, wrinkling back thin and bloodless lips to reveal long, discolored teeth most unpleasantly.

"I know naught of this 'cricket' you speak of, foreign devil," Alibeck hissed, "neither do I give a fig for what is or is not done in the best of circles!"

"Dashed rude blighter, this, what?" remarked Mandricardo to Sir Blundamore. Overhearing his words, the Wicked Wizard gave utterance to a mocking cackle of laughter.

"I know not, nor can I guess, how you penetrated the secret of the Topless Tower, thus breaking the spell where so many others have failed to do so," said Alibeck venomously. "But you and your companions will gain little from the feat, for where once a Topless Tower has stood, imprisoning one, a second can be raised capacious enough to hold *five* prisoners in durance—"

"Oh, now, I say, old chap! That's simply not playing fair," said Mandricardo indignantly. "Unfreeze my feet and let us have it out, sword to sword—!"

Alibeck favored him with another of those nasty, sneering grins in which he seemed to specialize.

"No Wicked Wizard ever got anywhere in this world by playing fair," he pointed out—and not without a considerable amount of logic on the side of his argument, villain or no villain—"so you may as well throw down your swords, all of you, and surrender. They would prove but of little or no avail against sorcery such as mine!"

"*Dashed* if I will!" blustered Mandricardo, virtuously. "The laws of chivalry—"

"Oh, *blast* these precious laws of chivalry you prate of," snarled the Wicked Wizard peevishly. He was beginning to get seriously exasperated by this stubborn, pigheaded fool of a Tartar, who simply did not seem to know when he was licked.

Sir Mandricardo looked shocked; Callipygia gasped indignantly; Blundamore glared at the enchanter, and, as for Sir Malaprop, he fixed the Wicked Wizard with a look of frosty reproof, and said, "Now, you just see here, me good felly! One simply cannot go around, what, speaking in such a tone of the laws of chivalry. Why, hell's bones, me good man—!"

Alibeck would probably have thrown up his hands in despair of ever getting through to these unrepentent captives, had not he been holding his wandful of wriggling vipers in one of them.*

"I've no patience left to discuss these matters with the likes of you," snapped Alibeck. "And I've changed my plans—instead of clapping the lot of you into durance vile atop another of my Topless Towers, I'll simply turn you all into stones."

"Or *toads*," he added meditatively. "Yes, on the whole, I think *toads* would be best." He then, rather shockingly, uttered what can only be called a gig-

---

*One of his *hands*, I mean.

gle. "People *do* so hate being transformed into toads," he remarked, with a dreamy smile.

And he raised his snaky wand and pointed it at them.

And just at that moment a hoarse, whiskey-roughened voice spoke from directly behind where he stood.

"Oh, foosh, mon! Yere endless gabble-gabble-gabble is keepin' a far better mon than yereself from his well-desairved rest!"

This unexpected voice-out-of-nowhere took Alibeck completely by surprise. He had not noticed till now that Braggadochio was curled up in slumber under a mulberry bush. The shock to his poor nerves was such that he uttered a strangled yelp and leaped about four inches into the air.

When he came down, as it happened, he landed on a loose stone, which rolled under his carpet slipper, pitching him on his back. He hit the ground with a resounding *thump*, which not only knocked the air out of him, but which also jarred the magic wand from his hand. It clattered to earth a couple of yards away.

The moment it touched the ground, the enchantment which held Mandricardo and Blundamore frozen to the earth was broken. The blond young knight—for once moving with agility and even grace—sprang forward, with great presence of mind, to kick the magical implement well out of Alibeck's reach.

"Ker-*hem!*" observed Sir Malaprop, adjusting his little spectacles on his nose. "A very well timed interruption, 'pon my word! Sort of puts this magician felly at a bit of a disadvantage, heh?"

"Yes, well done, well done, sir!" exclaimed

Mandricardo, and his lady-love and Princess Angelica joined in the chorus of praise. Pinking at this rare burst of approval, Braggadochio took a hasty swig from his bottomless black jug—if only to restore him to his natural aplomb—and essayed a rather uneven and wobbly bow.

"A-weel," he said modestly, twirling the ends of his walrus mustache, "I kenned it weel that 'twas time to interrupt the dommed braying jockoss, and did wha' any knight wud 've done, onder the ceercumstonces—"

Just then Callipygia yipped and snatched up her bow.

"Look out!" she cried.

They whirled to see that Alibeck the Avaricious had clambered shakily to his feet and was giving them the benefit of another of those toothy leers of his.

"Think you've won the contest, don't you?" he hissed, and reached out one hand with a beckoning gesture—

Whereupon, the wand that had fallen from his hand a few moments ago, lifted itself uncannily off the ground and flew through the air. Its smooth wooden handle slapped against his palm and his clawlike fingers closed about the haft.

"Now, let me see," mused the Wicked Wizard thoughtfully, "Where were we before this drunken scarecrow interrupted our discourse? Oh, yes . . . stones or toads. On the whole, I prefer toads—so deliciously slimy, warty and squishy!"

Our heroes can hardly be criticized for wilting a bit. It looked hopeless. "Should have smashed the bally old wand to flinders when we had the chance," muttered Sir Mandricardo to himself, disgustedly.

"Mustn't blame yourself, Mandro," said Blundamore stoutly. "Can't think of everything, you know. Stiff upper lip, that's the way!"

As for Callipygia, she crossed her arms on her chest, lifted her firm little chin in the air with stubborn defiance, and fixed the Wicked Wizard with a cold, accusing glare. One of her hands just happened to be restlessly fiddling with the thick bronze ring she wore clasped about her upper arm.

"You are a worm!" she said to Alibeck, flatly.

So of course he was . . .

Quite understandably, under the circumstances, the adventurers stared about them in baffled amazement. And none of them noticed the small pink worm that scuttled timidly from underfoot, to lose itself in the grass.

"Now, where d'you suppose that dastardly wizard has gotten himself to?" demanded Sir Mandricardo. It was a question which none of those present could answer—nor can I, for that matter. but wherever the worm, which was all that remained of Alibeck the Avaricious, did in fact get himself to, he never bothered any of them again, nor, for that matter, anybody else . . . unless, just possibly, his brother-worms.

Once a villain, always a villain, you know.

There sounded a sharp *crack!* as Alibeck's magic wand shattered itself into seven pieces, which lapsed into so many pinches of dry dust. As for the vipers, they were happy to wriggle away into the woods.

"Why, look!" cried Angelica, pointing one rosy-tipped finger. "The magic barrier of thorns . . ."

As they watched, the wall of bristling barbs, deprived of the Wicked Wizard's now-broken power, which alone sustained them in their magical existence, withered and dried up, and fell to ash which the cool breeze of early evening blew away. And the pass through the hills which led back into the kingdom of Sangaranga, no longer blocked, lay open to them.

Since the rescue of Angelica was now effected to their satisfaction, they resolved to follow their original plan, leaving Braggadochio and Sir Malaprop behind to guard the ransom of Angelica, while the others returned to the city astride the Steed of Brass to apprise stout little King Akbad of these eventualities, which, they knew, would delight his heart.

As night had now fallen, they proceeded about their tasks with all alacrity. None of them had eaten a bite since noon, and they were eager for even the sort of meager meal the Castle Cook would undoubtedly serve up—and cold to boot, at this hour! Still, gruel was gruel and mush was mush, and better a mouthful of *something*, than a mouthful of nothing.

The picnic hamper and the rolled-up Magic Flying Carpet safely stored aboard in the capacious cargo-space situated in the hollow haunches of the Brazen Horse, Mandricardo and Callipygia, Blundamore and Angelica were preparing to climb upon the back of the mechanical marvel . . . when yet another unexpected interruption occurred.

Rosy light blossomed in the midst of the clearing where once had stood the topless tower. Petals of pink luminosity parted, as of a rose of light, to disclose, shimmering into view, the shape of a tall and stately woman with a severe but gracious beauty, wrapped in dark hooded robes of somber stuff. Cradled in her arms like a King's sceptre or a Fairy's magic wand this newcomer bore a branch of the whitethorn tree.

"Oh, I say, this is *too* much!" grumbled Sir Mandricardo to his Amazonian lady-love. "The way people just appear and then disappear in this bally kingdom is beginning to wear on my nerves . . . and whomever do you suppose *this* stern-looking creature will prove to be, what?"

"I haven't the slightest idea," whispered Callipygia in reply, "but, for now, *do* be quiet and let us see if we can find out!"

It seemed, however, that one of them, at least, was acquainted with the statuesque and dignified woman in the hooded robe, for Princess Angelica uttered a pretty little cry of happiness and rushed into the woman's arms and embraced her fondly.

"Why, *godmother!*" she exclaimed, "what a pleasure to see you again after all these long years—"

BOOK FIVE

The Secret
of
the Ring

21

The Fairy Whitethorn

The robed woman returned the girl's embrace with a mixture of tenderness and affection that was a pleasure to behold.

"Angelica, my dear! How well you look, and, my goodness gracious—*how* you have grown!" she exclaimed in rich and mellow tones. "If I did not know better, I would swear that you have thrived and virtually blossomed as a prisoner of that greedy villain, Alibeck . . ."

Then, gently disengaging herself from the embrace of the Princess, the tall woman turned to greet them with a quiet smile.

"I am the Fairy Whitethorn," she explained. "The guardian of the kingdom of Sangaranga (although a poor guardian I have proven to be, alas!), and godmother to dear little Angelica, whom I discover has grown into beauteous womanhood."

And without further ado, conjuring from thin air a thronelike chair of carven peachwood and seating herself thereupon, the Fairy summoned a sphere of glimmering luminosity, of a pale and

pearly hue, to illuminate the gloom-drenched glade,
for there was no moon at all that night, and the
darkness was such that it was all the adventurers
could do to see the hand before their face.* This
pearly glow waxed and waned like the beating of a
living heart, and was centered about the calm figure enthroned in the peachwood chair. Although
pallid, it served to relieve the gloom, and, as the
little band of adventurers seated themselves tailor-
fashion upon the greensward, the Fairy began to
relate the following account, which I will here
transcribe verbatim from the pages of the *Chronicle Narrative*.

"I was absent from the kingdom of Sangaranga
—the Fairy Whitethorn began her story—"upon a
certain matter of urgent Fairy business, which I
undertook on behalf of my dear and only sister,
the Fairy Blackstick. As Blackstick commonly resides
in a secluded vale between the kingdoms of
Paflagonia and Crim-Tartary, and as these realms
lay many thousands of leagues from here, in the
world's west, I was absent from Sangaranga for
quite some time, and out of touch with the march
of events here in King Akbad's country.

"Naturally, I thought nothing of this, as Sangaranga is—or was until recently—one of those sleepy,
quiet little kingdoms where nothing of any particular importance has ever happened . . . no wars,
insurrections, invasions, attacks by monsters, revo-
lutions, or other cataclysms. In my innocence, I
had expected Sangaranga to continue in this placid
path until such time as my business on the behalf

---

*Although why anybody should particularly want to see their
hand before their face has always puzzled me. Well, no matter.

of my dearest sister was concluded and I was able to return to this country and once again assume the burden of my fairy-guardianship, which I had temporarily been forced, by the swift tide of events, to set down.

"As you must all be well aware, it was during this interval that the rascally Alibeck appeared to press his vile demands upon the monarch and populace of the kingdom, the which he enforced by carrying off into a secret place known only to himself my darling godchild, Angelica.

"You mortals may very well be unaware of this fact, but the magical powers of a guardian-fairy such as myself are directly linked to the prosperity and happiness and well-being of the citizens of that nation over which the Fairy Queen has appointed her the wardenship of; and by the time I was able to return to poor Sangaranga and to resume my duties, the kingdom was already bled white by Alibeck the Avaricious. The people had lapsed into listless poverty; starvation was rife; fields and farms, gardens and groves lay waste and fallow; game had deserted the fields and fish had fled the streams of Sangaranga, and the King himself dwelt in a dire and shabby state of poverty such, surely, as few reigning monarchs have endured.

"Thus it was that I found my own fairy powers drained and depleted. Although it was not difficult for me to discover the whereabouts of the Topless Tower in which the Wicked Wizard had cruelly imprisoned my darling goddaughter, his powers were far too great by now for me to challenge him to a magical duel. All I could do was to unobtrusively guide visiting knights and questing princes and suchlike stalwart champions to the hidden location of the Tower, hoping that by their wit, ingenuity or sheer luck they might be able to overcome Alibeck, break his dastardly spell, and set Princess Angelica free. But my help had to be all but invisible, so that not even Alibeck might become suspicious that I had returned and was secretly lending what little aid I could manage to the potential rescuers of the Princess—"

"Such," said Mandricardo cleverly, "as planting signs about, reading 'This Way to the Captive Princess,' I'll warrant, eh? What?"

The Fairy smiled warmly upon the Tartar knight, and nodded her head in regal manner.

"Precisely, good Sir Mandricardo! But such were the limitations set upon my depleted powers by fairy law that I could not even whisper in your ear the solution to the problem of bringing the Topless Tower down to earth again . . . although I *did* risk implanting in your mind this very noontime the precaution of packing the Magic Flying Carpet along with you when you and your knightly comrades were about to attempt to crush a path through the magical barrier of thornbushes Alibeck had raised to block every approach to this little vale."

"I suppose few other of the knights who tried and failed to rescue Angelica had much chance to succeed without something like the Carpet," murmured Callipygia.

The Fairy Whitethorn nodded. "That is true, my dear; one *did* arrive on a winged horse, though, and I had high hopes . . . ah, well! all's well that ends at all, and it was left to young Sir Blundamore, here, to guess the secret of undoing the enchantment."

Angelica bent a fond glance on the blond knight,

who blushed crimson and promptly fell over his feet.

"I can feel the magical power pouring back into my person, now that my darling little Angelica has been·set free, the Tower destroyed, Alibeck deprived of all his skill, and the national treasury of Sangaranga recovered seemingly intact," murmured the Fairy. As if to demonstrate the truth of her words, the pearly luminance which pulsed about her and served to illuminate the dark glade strengthened until it was nearly as brilliant as the light of day. The Fairy sighed.

"Ah, me! I became as poor as the very kingdom I was appointed to watch over and to ward from harm," she said. "So poor, in fact, that I have to pawn my very own magic wand over in the kingdom next door* and adopt the use of a branch of my namesake tree in place of it. Now that I have become accustomed to using the branch in lieu of my wand, I think I shall retain it as my trademark, so to speak. Do you find it becoming?"

They assured the Fairy that it was, indeed.

It was by now past midnight, and they were all exhausted with the perils and exertions of the day, and also hungry as starved bears, not having had their suppers. Now that her magic was returning, Whitethorn assured them it would be no difficulty for her to transport them all—yes, and Rosie, Blondel, and Bayardetto, too, as well as the Horse of Brass—back to the courtyard of King Akbad's castle in a twinkling. As for the treasure trove, it was simplicity itself for the powerful Fairy

*Whose name, you may remember, was "Nexdoria." I hate to throw away a good pun on a scant few mentions.

to cast a potent spell to protect it from theft or
molestation until next morning, when doubtless
King Akbad would be dispatching a caravan to
transport it all back to the capital.

These things were all accomplished in a trice.
They had to get the fat little King out of bed to
greet his daughter and her rescuers, and the Castle Cook went into a fit of hysterics, when she
learned there were six hungry mouths to feed—
but the Fairy Whitethorn swiftly conjured up a
groaning banquet table heavy-laden with steaming
platters of broiled trout, an entire roast boar smoking from every pore and swimming in giblet gravy,
mounds of delicious pastries so light they had to
be held down with paperweights lest they float up
to the ceiling, pyramids of ripe and dewy fruit,
three kinds of soup in solid gold tureens, nine
kinds of chilled wine, and enough vintage champagne to fill two or three bathtubs.

I assure you that the little kingdom of Sangaranga
had not known such a merry tableful of feasters in
years and years, despite the lateness of the hour,
and so many toasts were drunk in champagne that
when Mandricardo at last went stumbling off to his
bed, he barely had time to divest himself of his
armor before falling into bed, and was sound asleep
upon the very next instant.

The Tartar knight slept so very soundly that he
did not awaken until nearly noon. After a hot
bath and a hearty breakfast, he wandered out into
the weed-patch that had once been the royal rose
garden, and discovered to his satisfaction that it
had become a rose garden again. It seemed that,
once Alibeck's spell was broken and the kingdom

restored to its normal state, Nature smiled once
again on the Sangarangians.

From where he stood on the terrace, Mandricardo could see that the groves and vinyards were
literally exploding into bloom—as if hurriedly making up for lost time—and the farms and fields in
the distance, which had been parched and brown,
were green again and burgeoning with cabbages
and turnips and other vegetables.

From the number of fishermen clustered excitedly on the bridge and wading out into the river
in their hip-high gumboots, the Tartar knight
guessed (and quite correctly) that the trout and
salmon and turbot and suchlike had returned to
populate the lakes and rivers.

In short, Sangaranga was recovering from its
long infliction of drought, poverty, and malicious
enchantment. It did the heart of the knight-errant
good to behold this wondrous change.

Down the long road from the hills where the
Topless Tower had stood came groaning wainloads
full of treasure, closely guarded by the soldiery of
the realm, and from the other direction, in which,
he had been given to understand, lay Nexdoria,
came yet other caravans of wains filled to the brim
with foodstuffs purchased from the more fortunate Nexdorians by the merchants of Sangaranga,
now that their lost wealth had been restored. There
were wainloads of ham and veal and beef and
pork, and brace after brace of plump gamebirds,
and great wheels of cheese, and wagonsful of potatoes and onions and carrots and so on, while
other vehicles creaked gamely along, loaded with
barrels of wine and ale, baskets of eggs and fruit,
and mounds of fresh-baked bread. Today, the
happy, carefree Sangarangians would feast as they

had not feasted since the coming of Alibeck years
before.

Mandricardo grinned, and tweaked the corners
of his drooping mustache in great good humor.

"Jolly good, what? What?" said the Tartar to
himself.

22

Farewell to Sangaranga

Three days later Sir Blundamore and the Princess Angelica were married, and the happy occasion was marked with riotous festivities in which the peasants and townspeople joined in wholeheartedly. Now that the once-poor kingdom of Sangaranga, now richer than ever,* was blooming like a veritable garden, every furrow and branch and bush literally bursting with luscious fruit and nourishing vegetables, the citizenry were heartily enjoying banquets and feasts such as they had seldom known before.

Huge barrels of ale and wine stood at every street corner, on Blundamore's and Angelica's wedding night, and trestle tables had been set up

---

* This was because, when the Fairy Whitethorn told King Akbad where the late Alibeck's secret cavern was located, he at once dispatched a body of soldiers to the spot, in case there were captives to be released. Well, they didn't find any captives, I'm glad to say—but they did find lots and *lots* more treasure which, obviously, the greedy rascal had milked from other victims, before bothering Sangaranga.

in the streets, while every kitchen bustled with
lively activity. Hams and wild turkeys, boar and
whole sheep and huge haunches of venison and
beef, and enough trout and salmon to repopulate
half the rivers and lakes of Asia were turning on
the spit. Bread was baking, vegetables simmering,
tureens of soup were bubbling, and as the sun set
the merry Sangarangians enjoyed the hugest, most
unforgettable feast of their lives in honor of the
happy couple.

Up at the castle, of course, the nobles and gentry had a feast of their own. Ten thousand candles
turned dark into day, and long tables groaned
beneath the burden of good things to eat. Prince
Blundamore and *his blushing bride,* as you might
very well expect, had eyes only for each other,
and barely touched the many dishes that were set
before them. Oh, perhaps they nibbled on a bit of
salad or munched a steaming muffin or two, but
that was about the extent of their feasting.

During the interminable banquet, and smack in
the midst of one of the dullest speeches you may
ever have heard—it was by the Bishop—the young
couple crept out and departed on their honeymoon. Instead of the Riviera or the Greek Isles or
something exotic like that, they had determined to
spend their honeymoon in a secluded hunting
lodge in the hills which belonged to the royal
family of Sangaranga. They both left good-bye-
and-thanks notes for Mandricardo, Callipygia, and
the two older knights.

For the next few days, the adventurers just loafed
around the castle, snoozing summery afternoons
away in hammocks set up in the rose garden, or
conversing lazily with various of the court digni-
taries. While they rested up and enjoyed their lazy

little respite from long adventurings, the castle armorers tightened the bolts and screws on their armor, refurbished and polished and oiled the steel platework, gently tapped dents out of their helms, and hammered and filed nicks and missing chips from the blades of their swords.

Sir Malaprop, who was, of course, the eldest of the party, particularly enjoyed the rare luxury of sleeping in a real bed, for once, rather than camping out in the wilderness, under a dripping bush or whatever. His years of pursuing the Galumphing Beast had seldom afforded him much of an opportunity to slumber in a real feather bed, with plenty of plump goosedown pillows, and he was rapidly making up for lost time.

Erelong, however, Sir Mandricardo began to grow impatient to begone and on the road. The last leg of their journey to Tartary lay before them, and was likely to prove an extremely difficult and rugged experience. There were mountains in the way—and plenty of them, high ones, too—and fetid swamps and bubbling fens and savage jungles where doubtless prowled the scarlet Mantichore that delights in no sweeter dish than *human flesh,* and quite likely a Dragon or two would be encountered along the way, these parts of Hither Asia being well known for their Dragons.

And so the Tartar knight began to grow edgy, to fidget, and to suggest repeatedly that it was about time they got back in the saddle and on the road again. . . .

Actually, it was not very long before his companions also began to decide it was time to go.

They were, all of them—except, perhaps, for Sir Braggadochio—naturally modest, as modesty becomes heroes and champions and is one of their nicest virtues. And they had all about had it up to *here* with having to sit through lengthy speeches of praise, and the recitation of heroic victory odes written in their honor, and laying cornerstones, and launching boats, and being cheered and fêted and feasted wherever they went.

Callipygia put it this way one afternoon: "If I have to pose for a statue, or have my portrait painted, or sign *just one more autograph*, I swear, Mandro, I shall scream, or run wild, or take the veil, or—something!"

And so, at length, it was decided; and, without further ado, they saddled up, loaded their gear aboard the Horse of Brass, and bright and early the very next morning, after a sumptuous breakfast with ham, bacon *and* sausages, and both toast *and* hot biscuits, and three kinds of fruit juice, and scrambled eggs *and* pancakes, they left the country of Sangaranga, and rode through cheering crowds while from every rooftop flowers pelted down upon their heads like a snowstorm incongruously met with in midsummer.

Once they were beyond the borders of the little kingdom, and found themselves in the hills to the east, Sir Mandricardo heaved a deep and heartfelt sigh of relief.

"Feels bally good to be back in the saddle and about our journey again, what?" he asked in cheerful tones. "Enough of lolling about comfy castles, wallowing in slothful indolence, with lackeys scurrying to obey your slightest whim—*that's* no life for a bally knight-errant, eh?"

Braggadochio, who would have been perfectly happy to have stayed behind in Sangaranga, indefinitely enjoying the Sangarangian hospitality

and the measureless contents of his magical little
black jug, whuffled through his bristle of red
mustache and remarked *sotto voce* something more
or less to the effect of "speak for yereself, me
gude mon!", but as his comment was phrased in
Gaelic (or whatever it was), the Tartar knight paid
no attention.

"Yes, indeed!" exclaimed Callipygia, gazing
around her. The sky was clear and blue and cloud-
less; larks, or whatever they were, were singing to
beat the band in every blossoming tree; the sun
was rich and golden overhead; and the long wind-
ing road to Tartary and home lay ahead of them.

It looked like it was going to be a beautiful day.

"Ker-*hem*," said Sir Malaprop, a trifle wistfully.
"Can't say as how I'm not going to miss that feather
bed. Hell's bones, if I'm not!"

"Never you mind, my dear old chap," advised
Sir Mandricardo cheerily. "We have plenty of
feather beds up in Tartary, you know—"

Sir Malaprop, who hadn't known, looked a bit
more perky at the news.

"Good, deep, soft ones?" he inquired hopefully.

"Softer than a snowbank, by my halidom!"

"Would there be plenty of plump little down
pillows, do you suppose, my good felly?"

"As many as your heart desires," Mandricardo
assured him. "You have my word."

"'Pon my soul," marveled Sir Malaprop—who
knew about as much about Tartary as probably
you do.*

And, chatting in friendly fashion between themselves, the little party of adventurers rode on into
the splendid morning.

---

*Or, for that matter, me.

"Did I tell you that Dame Whitethorn gave me a little present, before we left?" murmured Callipygia to her betrothed. She produced the gift, a small tube of fretted silver with a screw-top at one end.

"That's nice," he said. "What is it?"

She unscrewed the top and shook out on her palm one slim, sharp white thorn from the Fairy's branch, or wand, or whatever you prefer to call it.

"Ah? Bit of a keepsake, what? Souvenir, I think they call 'em . . ."

The Amazon girl shook her head.

"Bit more than that, actually," she informed him. "It has some magic, I gather. The Fairy Whitethorn gave it to me, saying that perhaps sometime I might need to talk to her or to ask her advice on something. So, if I ever do, all I have to do is snap the magic thorn in two and she promises to appear wherever I may happen to be at the time."

"How very thoughtful of the old gel," said Mandricardo absently, watching a flight of geese and thinking of the luscious goose-liver paté the Castle Cook had stowed away in the picnic hamper at his hint.

And they rode on . . . never guessing just how soon the magic thorn from the Fairy's wand was going to come in handy.

Beyond the hills lay a range of mountains, and they selected what seemed to be the easiest pass through them.

Before long they came to a place where the pass narrowed somewhat, and here they encountered a barrier of sorts. Well, it wasn't *much* of a barrier—true—just a rusty old chain that stretched from one side of the mountain wall to the other. But it was meant for a barrier, and that was all that counted. They dismounted to examine it more closely, and Sir Mandricardo discovered an old, peeling sign by the side of the road, half overgrown with bushes. The lettering had been painted on, quite obviously, a very long time ago, and years of wind and sun and rain and weather had nearly erased the notice. But not entirely.

The sign read:

NOW ENTERING FEMENYE.
No m. . . allowed!

Mandricardo read this to the others; unfortunately the second word in the bottom line was almost illegible, save for the first letter. They wondered what the missing word might be.

"Magicians?" suggested Callipygia. "If they're this close to Sangaranga, they might very well decide to forbid entry into their country to all magicians."

"*Monsters*, mebbe? Kaff?" This from Sir Malaprop, who had paused to light the stump of his cigar butt with that handy little Ever-Burning Coal the enchanter had given him, long ago.

". . . Femenye . . . Femenye . . . doesn't ring a bell with me, what? Any of you chaps ever hear of the place?" inquired the Tartar knight. The two older men shook their heads.

"This is one of those times we could certainly use that handy Gazetteer Sir Blundamore always carried with him," said Callipygia in thoughtful tones. "Pity it never occurred to any of us to borrow it from him . . . for, now that he's married, I don't expect he will do much more riding about the world on quests and adventures."

"Raw*ther!*" chuckled Sir Mandricardo, a roguish twinkle in his dark eye. "Stayin' home, tendin' to business, and raisin' plenty of fat babies, more like! Eh, m'love?" he grinned, giving the Amazon girl a suggestive nudge in the ribs.

Callipygia turned pink and said nothing. But she *did* simper, just a little.

"Might as well have some lunch, what?" suggested Malaprop, and indeed the sun stood at the zenith and a brisk morning's ride in the fresh open air had given them all an appetite, huge breakfast under their belts or no huge breakfast under their belts.

They unsaddled their steeds and let them roam at will and crop what little verdure grew here and there, waiting to be cropped, while Mandricardo hauled down the picnic basket from the hollow haunches of the Horse and Callipygia spread out a tablecloth beside the road.

23

The Spell of Sleep

Their lunch was a far more sumptuous repast than had been the meager contents of the last picnic basket the Castle Cook had prepared for them, when they were on their way to discover the Topless Tower and to rescue Angelica. There was broiled peacock with chestnut stuffing, potato salad with dill and mayonnaise dressing, tomatoes stuffed with cheese and chopped olives, six bottles of chilled champagne, a selection of luscious fruits, sliced cheese and ham, and a jar of sour pickles. For desert, there were strawberry tarts.

The travelers made short work of this roadside feast, repacked the scraps and remnants in the picnic basket, stored it away again in the hollow haunches of the Steed of Brass, and prepared to enter the country of Femenye, of which none of them had ever heard. It *sounded* like an unfriendly place, from that sign beside the entrance to the pass, but that couldn't be helped.

"After all, dash it, what," said Sir Mandricardo,

"we're harmless travelers just passing through, you know."

They unfastened one end of the chain which, however inadequately, served to bar their passage, and their steeds stepped over it as they entered the pass.

However, they had not gotten twenty yards into the country of Femenye,* before they had good reason to understand just how truly *in*hospitable the Femenyites really were . . .

It was Sir Malaprop who was the first to discover this hostility on the part of the citizenry of Femenye to uninvited visitors, harmless or no.

He suddenly turned the pin which brought the Horse of Brass to a complete halt. Then he stretched his arms out and gave vent to a jaw-cracking yawn. Blinking his vague blue eyes sleepily, he mumbled, "Dashed sleepy all of a sudden, you know. Kaff! Take a little nap, I think . . ."

And with those surprising words, the bald little knight sort of curled up in the capacious saddle of the magical Steed and fell sound asleep!

Sir Mandricardo pulled back on the reins of his black charger, and removed his steel helm. "Bally good idea, that," he murmured. "Believe I could do with a bit of a snooze, myself . . ."

And he promptly fell off Bayardetto's back, rolled off the road into the grass, and began snoring lustily.

As for Sir Braggadochio, he simply fell over backward off his bony nag and landed in the middle of the road with a crash of jangling, rusty

* Presuming, that is, that the chain and sign marked the border of the country.

armor. But by now Callipygia was so used to him
falling out of the saddle, that she hardly noticed.

The Amazon girl stared at her fallen friends,
eyes wide with astonishment. "By Hercules' hang-
nail," she muttered to herself, "what's all *this*?"

Her first thought was that Alibeck the Avaricious had popped up again and was taking his
vengeance upon those who had brought about his
downfall. But that was hardly likely. For one thing,
he would not have spared Callipygia herself from
that vengeance; and for another, he would not
have been satisfied *at all* with just sending the
knights into slumberland . . . when last heard from,
the Wicked Wizard had decided to turn them all
into cold, slimy, warty, squishy toads. . . .

Callipygia dismounted from Blondel and tried
to awaken Sir Mandricardo. She took a canteen
of water from the storage-space in the haunches
of the Brazen Steed and dashed the cold liquid in
his face. He only rolled over and began to snore
even more loudly than before. She slapped his
face until her palms turned bright pink and began
to sting—she yelled in his ear—but nothing was of
any avail.

The Tartar knight refused to awaken.

It just *had* to be a magic spell. There was no
getting around it, such a sudden—and *infectious*—
fit of sleepiness was far from being natural.

And, if it wasn't the work of the villainous Alibeck
(and it certainly didn't seem to be, for the reasons
given above), then the culprits could only be the
unfriendly, and so far *unseen*, people of Femenye.

But, if so, where were they? Why didn't they
attack, or something? Carry them off captives, or
whatever?

Callipygia could find no answer to any of these
puzzling questions. She resolved to sit down and
wait; perhaps the fit of sudden sleep was a natural
phenomenon, and, with time, would pass. So she
removed the bit and bridle and saddle from their
horses, not forgetting frisky little Minerva the mule,
and let them crop the greensward, while she
perched on a nearby boulder in the cool shade of
the cliffwall, and . . . waited.

And . . . *waited.*

And . . . *WAITED.*

But the three stricken knights snoozed on.

After some little time, Callipygia got up and began to pace to and fro. She felt fidgety and yearned
to go into action: but she couldn't think of any
action she could take that would accomplish anything. There is probably nothing in the world
more sheerly frustrating than to need desperately
to do *something* to alleviate an intolerable situation,
without having the slightest idea of exactly *what* to
do.

And then, all of a sudden, the Amazon girl
thought of the magic thorn the Fairy Whitethorn
had given her just before she had left the kingdom of Sangaranga with the trio of champions
who now lay at her feet, snoozing away blissfully
as so many babes.

Well, she could almost have kicked herself, had
such a thing been anatomically possible. Of *course!*
The good Fairy had said that sometime or other
Callipygia might very well need to consult her, ask
her advice or beg her help—and *this* was certainly
the time she needed the help of a friendly Fairy!

The Amazon girl took out the silver filigree

case and removed the magic thorn therefrom. Taking a deep breath, she snapped the dry thorn in two ... and waited to see what would happen next.

What happened next was a slow burst of rosy light whose petals unfolded like those of a rose of fire, to reveal the serene figure of Angelica's Fairy Godmother. She looked exactly as she had when Callipygia had last seen her, and exactly as she would still look a hundred years from now and more, since Fairies do not change very much over the years. Her expression was grave, her eyes searching, her mouth stern but tender.

"Well, child! I had not thought that you would be calling upon my help quite *this* quickly," said the Fairy, "but I am always happy to help a friend in trouble. But, tell me, daughter—what sort of trouble are you in this time?"

Callipygia gestured wordlessly at the three sleeping figures sprawled on the ground, and in a few short words explained what had happened.

To her surprise, the Fairy began to laugh!

It was the first time in their acquaintance that Callipygia had heard the Fairy Whitethorn laugh (usually she seemed calm and detached and of placid temperament), and she may be forgiven, I think, if she stared.

Whitethorn wiped her eyes on a corner of her sleeve, and smiled at the Amazon girl.

"You will have to forgive me, my dear," she said, "but, after all, don't you know where you are?"

Calipygia blinked. "In Femenye," she said.

Angelica's Fairy Godmother nodded regally.

"Quite correct; in Femenye. And what do you know about Femenye?"

"Why, nothing at all!" cried Callipygia. The Fairy looked rather surprised.

"Is that a fact, my dear? Goodness me, you are from Amazonia, and yet you know nothing about the country of Femenye?"

"No, I don't," said Callipygia in puzzled tones.

The Fairy Whitethorn shrugged slightly.

"Well, no matter . . . I will save my explanations until we have revived your companions from their magical slumbers, so as not to have to repeat the story a second time. First we must get them back in the saddles of their steeds, and then we must lead their horses by the bridle. Once we have crossed the borders of Femenye, they will awaken, having taken no harm from their experience, I assure you . . ."

"But—!"

"Come, my dear," help me resaddle the charger, and then, together, I think we can lift your Tartar friend back into the saddle, despite the weight of his armor."

Callipygia bit her lip and did as she was told.

While the Fairy Whitethorn led Rosie and Bayardetto by their bridles out of the pass, with their masters swaying across the withers of the horses—I *think* I mean withers—and with Blondel and Miranda trotting obediently behind, Callipygia, on top of the Horse of Brass (and holding onto Sir Malaprop with one hand, lest he fall from the back of the miraculous machine, guided the Steed with her other hand on the control pin.

And, no sooner had they all stepped across the chain in the road, than the Spell of Sleep was broken!

"Ker-hem! Hakk!" remarked Sir Malaprop, sitting up and yawning and looking about him perplexedly. "Hell's bones," he said, "did I sleep all night in me armor? Felly could get the rheumatiz doin' that ... cold mornin' dew, you know ... and what am I doin' here in the saddle?"

"Never mind," said Callipygia fondly.

Mandricardo had also aroused from his slumbers. He yawned and stretched and blinked about him. "Lovely morning, what," he remarked drowsily. "Seem to have gone to sleep with all my armor on. What time is it, anyway? Sun seems dashed high in the sky for it to be very early—"

Then he noticed the Fairy Whitethorn, and frowned in puzzlement.

"I say, what's toward, eh? Cally? What's been happening? By my halidom, I smell vile enchantments and all that sort of thing ... chap doesn't just go to sleep in the saddle, what, fully dressed and all ..."

"Everything's all right now," Callipygia assured him.

As for Braggadochio, he restored his nerves with a hefty belt of the potent restorative contained in the bottomless little black jug.

"If you all care to dismount, I will explain what happened to you," suggested the Fairy.

Her audience disposed themselves upon conveniently-placed boulders, and the Fairy, conjuring out of nothingness that carved and thronelike chair of hers, seated herself within, laying her magic thornbranch-wand in her lap.

"Femenye," she began, "was founded by distant relatives of dear Callipygia, here; that is, by cousins of ancestors of hers. Since Amazonia in Pontus was becoming overcrowded, a certain tribe of Amazon women decided to move further east and establish another nation of their own, which they did, calling it Femenye.

"Now, doctrinal differences divided the two tribes. Whereas Callipygia's ancestors were willing to at least tolerate men as husbands and fathers, and were even capable of falling in love with them, the members of the second nation were rabidly against all males, and could not endure having any of the opposite sex around.

"Their Queen, as it happened, was a powerful sorceress, and, once they had founded the new nation, she cast a great spell upon the borders of Femenye so that any man or boy unfortunate or misguided enough to stray within its borders should fall into an enchanted slumber from which he could only be awakened by being dragged or carried back across those borders again and into the outside world, where the spell no longer had any effect. If this was not done, the unfortunate male would sleep forever."

Mandricardo turned pale and gulped. "I say, you chaps," he said feebly. "D'you realize that, if it hadn't been for Cally, here, being with us and able to summon help, we'd all have slept right there in the bally road till . . . doomsday?"

"Hell's bones," observed Sir Malaprop feebly.

"Oh, gude losh . . . sleep ain life awa' . . . so far, far fra' hame!" groaned Sir Braggadochio, and promptly took a good long swallow from that bottomless black jug of his, in order to steady his nerves.

After a moment, recovering himself, a thought occurred to Mandricardo. He cleared his throat.

"I say, madam, but . . . without men around . . . ahem! . . . I mean . . . ah, how could the dashed country keep goin', what?" he inquired delicately. "I mean to say, what, there is one thing men can do that, ah ... women can't ... if you take my meanin', ma'm," he finished lamely.

The Fairy Whitethorn smiled sadly.

"You are quite right, my friend," she said gravely. "And without men to father their children, the entire nation of Femenye died out within one generation, and is now long since extinct."

24

ZZZZYYTPX

Sir Mandricardo at length heaved a heartfelt sigh. "Well, you chaps, no hope for it, you know. We shall simply have to go around these bally mountains. I mean to say, can't risk goin' back into this dashed country of Femenye and gettin' put to sleep again, what?"

"Hem!" remarked Sir Malaprop, pursing his lips. "Don't suppose we could just fly *over* the mountains on your Magic Flyin' Carpet, young felly? Hell's bones, it'd take us *weeks* to travel around all these dashed mountains . . ."

The Tartar knight looked tempted, but shook his head with obvious reluctance.

"Daren't chance it, old top! Bally Carpet's worn and threadbare and about to rip in several places . . . the four of us, all our armor and luggage, the two horses and the mule—to say nothin' of the Brazen Steed, which must weigh a few tons, you know . . . daren't risk it," he decided gloomily.

"Kaff! Perhaps in several trips, heh?" suggested

223

Malaprop polishing his little spectacles vigorously on one corner of his pocket-handkerchief.

Mandricardo looked dubious. "We don't know anything about the countries beyond these mountains, what? Hate to split our party up . . . might not be all that safe. Wyverns and Basilisks and wild Mantichores and Griffins and whatnot . . . blighters teem like vermin in these parts of Asia, you know, old chap!"

"Um," said the bald, elderly little knight, licking his lips and staring unhappily at the end of his cigar, which had gone out.

The two knights looked over to Braggadochio, to see if he had anything of substance to contribute to this conversation, but the red-nosed man in the walrus mustache (who had been solacing his tummy with a dozen or so postprandial swigs from that bottomless black jug of his, was not listening, or not very closely, at least.

You can't very easily follow a discussion when you are singing *"Scots wha hae wi' Wallace bled"* under your breath, and keeping time all the while by punctuating each line with a well-timed hiccup.

"Head either north or south, I suppose, don't you think?" murmured Sir Mandricardo. "North would be best, since Tartary lies in that direction, don't you know. Dashed shame this Femenye place takes up so much room, but no help for it, what? Simply have to go the long way around, and that's that . . ."

Sir Mandricardo and Sir Malaprop, discussing the logistics of the proposed journey, strolled off arm in arm down the slope of the pass just a little, to be able to obtain a clear and unobstructed view of the terrain. They needed to pick the smoothest and shortest path north around the mountains—

the *Chronicle Narrative* doesn't say what the name of the mountains was, nor does Sir John de Mandeville give them a name on his map of this part of the East, so we shall just have to call them The Mountains, and leave it at that.

It is very much to be doubted if Sir Braggadochio even bothered to notice that the two of them had left him alone with the Amazon girl and Princess Angelica's Fairy Godmother. He had lost his place in singing *"Scots wha hae"* and thus had to go back to the beginning and start the song all over again.

By now it was getting into early afternoon and clouds were beginning to pile up against the west. They looked rather dark and disagreeable, those clouds, and from time to time there sounded in the distance from their depths those unpleasant digestive-sort-of noises that storm clouds often make. You know what I mean, I guess—not exactly thunder, but instead a sort of discreet rumbling as of an empty tummy wishing some food would come sliding down the old esophagus,* or whatever it is that they call that tube that begins at your mouth—you know—and ends up at the beginning of your digestive system.

In a word, it rather looked quite as though it might rain sometime before nightfall. . . .

Now, while Sir Mandricardo and Sir Malaprop were deeply engaged in their discussion of the serious business of which would be the shortest, best and easiest route for them to take on their journey around the mountains which walled in enchantment-guarded Femenye, the two women,

---

* I think I mean "esophagus," but I can't be bothered stopping to look the word up now, and, anyway, you know what I mean.

Callipygia and the Fairy Whitethorn, were busily talking about whatever-in-the-world-it-is that women talk about—when they are not talking about recipes, men, or babies, that is. Which is most of the time.

The Amazon girl had managed to overhear enough of the conversation the men were having to look worried. The long, long road they must take to circle all the way around these mountains looked rough and dusty and would certainly prove tiresome.

She said as much to her companion, during an interval in their little chat.

"Oh, dear, I *wish* we dared use the Carpet to carry all of us over these cursed mountains that stand so obstinately in our way!" Callipygia sighed. "I've had enough of tramping down rocky roads by now, and would dearly *love* to get to Tartary . . ."

The Fairy looked at her with an air of mild surprise, and pursed her lips a little.

"I have been rather meaning to ask you something, my dear," said Whitethorn tentatively, "although it is really none of my business, after all. But it has been puzzling me and nagging at me, since first I saw you . . ."

"What is it?"

"Well . . . as I say, my dear, it's certainly none of *my* business, but . . . why in the world do you go on taking the hard way over your difficulties, and the various dangers and obstacles which you find in your path, instead of simply wishing your way out of them?"

Callipygia looked at the good Fairy blankly.

". . . Instead of what?" she queried.

"I mean to say, well, after all, you *do* bear Aeskja Hrinja the Great, and you must certainly know how to use it by now!" said the Fairy Whitethorn. "That is to say, why, a child of *ten*—"

". . . Whatever are you talking about, Madam Whitethorn?" inquired the Amazon girl.

The Fairy godmother nodded at the old, battered bronze band which Callipygia had found weeks and weeks ago, back in the Troll's cave, and which she had worn ever since clasped about her biceps like an armlet.

"That ring, the Troll's ring," explained the Fairy simply. "Surely you must know it is a wishing ring, and one of the most famous and powerful of its kind ever fabricated by Dwarvish magic and skill."

It would not be an overstatement on my part to tell you that Callipygia literally *reeled*.*

". . . A *wishing ring*. . . ?" she repeated, her voice suddenly gone hoarse because her throat had just become very, very dry.

The Fairy Whitethorn nodded. "Why, of course, my dear! I would have mentioned it much earlier, but, well, goodness—I surely thought you must know all about it, and if you did not care to employ the powers of Aeskja Hrinja, well, that was of course your own private business, and it would be perhaps indelicate of me to pry into your privacy with my questions."

". . . N-no, I didn't know, as a m-matter of fact," whispered Callipygia, who by now had gone quite pale.

"Is that a fact," Dame Whitethorn marveled. "I should have thought by *this* time . . . well; at any rate; the Mastersmith of the Dwarves fashioned Aeskja Hrinja as a gift for the King of the Trolls.

---

* Although it is very difficult to reel while you are sitting down on a boulder, as the Amazon happened to be at the time.

This was *ever* so long ago, you understand, and I fear that it has quite gone out of my mind which Troll King it was—not that it really matters."

She reached over and traced the rude, uncouth runes cut in the band of old, age-darkened bronze which encircled Callipygia's muscular upper arm.

"These runes are in Trollish, of course, and spell out the word of transformation which, in Trollish magic, is 'Zzzzyytpx.' In order to change something into something else, all you have to do is to pronounce the word in that manner. To change it back, simply pronounce the word backward, or 'Xptyyzzzz.' Simplicity itself, wouldn't you say, my dear?

"Or," the Fairy added, "you can wish for whatever you most desire by simply twisting the ring back and forth upon your finger—if, that is, you are a Troll, whose finger would be as big about as is your arm."

"I have been wearing a wishing ring all this time, then," murmured Callipygia in hollow tones, suddenly feeling the urge to borrow Sir Braggadochio's fat little black jug for a moment and restore her tissues with a good healthy swig therefrom.

"Yes, I guess you have," said the Fairy. Then she continued, conversationally, "Everyone lost sight of Aeskja Hrinja, oh, ages and ages ago! And, since the Trolls no longer have a King, I suppose nobody bothered to go looking for it . . . interesting and rather amusing that you should have stumbled on it, and not even have known what it was that you had found!"

And the Fairy Whitethorn laughed merrily at the very thought. Callipygia, on the other hand, gritted her teeth.

"Then, back in the cave, when Mandro was complaining so about the cold and the wet and wished to be in a warm, dry climate, and I said, 'Well, I wish you were,' or words to that effect—?"

"Precisely," said the Fairy.

"And, a little while later, when I found myself on the edge of that great chasm, with no way to get across, and wished that I was a thousand leagues from that spot . . ."

"Quite certainly," said the Fairy.

"And," said Callipygia, skipping over the next few occasions, "just the other day when I got so peeved at that rascally Alibeck that I told him *he was a worm*—"

"Absolutely," said the Fairy. "And I must say, good riddance!"

And then, Dame Whitethorn changed the subject and began to chat about another matter entirely—and never afterward could the Amazon girl remember what it was, for she was not paying any attention.

Instead, she was staring dazedly off into the hazy distance, with the most peculiar and indescribable expression upon her face. Her eyes seemed watering into tears, and yet, at one and the same time, something very like a rueful little smile was tugging at the corners of her generous mouth. In truth, Callipygia did not know whether to laugh or to weep. But, on the whole, she did not think it would be very wise to laugh, for she had the inner conviction that once she start laughing it would be *quite* a while before she would be able to stop.

Shortly thereafter, Mandricardo and Sir Malaprop came strolling back up the slope of the mountain pass to where they had left the two women talking. Mandricardo was speaking to the older knight as they came ambling into earshot.

". . . So we are agreed, then, old chap, we take that straight path as far as the grassy knoll, then veer off to the left a bit, where the bally road curves about that spire of rock—then on, northerly and easterly, until we reach that huge hill . . ."

He broke off as they came up to where Callipygia and the Fairy Whitethorn were sitting.

"Ah, there you are, m'love, what?" said the Tartar knight amiably. "Sir Malaprop and I were just discussin' the best route we might take to get around these dashed mountains in our way, and we've decided—"

"Never mind all that now, dear," said Callipygia in firm tones. "It won't be needed. Dame Whitethorn has just, ah, informed me of a . . . shortcut . . . we can take, which will get us home to Tartary *much* quicker and easier. Like, for instance, in time to wash up before having dinner with your royal father and all your brothers."

Mandricardo's mouth fell open. Then, seeing the steely expression in the eyes of his betrothed, he closed it again.

"Well, ah, very well, of course, m'love, what. I mean, whatever you say, and all, but are you *really certain*—?"

"Just mount up, and help Braggadochio into the saddle. He seems to have fallen asleep again. Come along, come along!" said the Amazon girl.

Mandricardo exchanged a wondering glance with Sir Malaprop, who went 'Ker-haff, ker-hem!" as was his way, and averted his gaze. His cigar had gone out again and he pressed the magical Ever-

Burning Coal against the charred end of it and puffed the vile-smelling thing into life again.

"M'dear, are you *really sure*—" began Mandricardo. But Callipygia was in no mood for any further chitchat. She got up from her boulder and dusted off the back of her mail-skirt.

"Trust me," she said, briefly.

25

Happily Ever After!

After satisfying her thirst and her appetite at the dinner-feast, Callipygia wandered out into the walled gardens which surrounded the huge, ancient and rambling castle of King Agricane. After all the noise and wild music and whirling confusion and fireblaze of the enormous, high-raftered old hall, it was pleasant and refreshing to feel the cool breeze against your flushed cheeks and to realize that it had blown for endless leagues upon long leagues across the bleak steppes of High Tartary, and to see the sleeping roses nodding in the moonlight.

King Agricane had welcomed them with open arms, for not only was Sir Mandricardo the oldest of his seventeen tall and stalwart sons, and the heir presumptive to the Throne of Tartary, but also the son of his loins who happened to be dearest to his heart. The Amazon girl had fallen in love with the magnificent old man from the first, all seven feet of him, with those piercing black eyes and nose like a scimitar-blade, and those imposing silver mustaches, stiff as broomstraws, and obviously the King's pride and joy, from the way he constantly preened them.

The feast he had commanded for that evening, in order to celebrate most properly and in a fitting manner the return from his questings and adventures of the Prince of Tartary and his intended bride—Tartary's future Queen—was quite a shindig. Whole oxen were roasted on great spits above roaring bonfires, and there were stews and soups and ragouts enough to drown grown men in, and mountains of crisp, flaky vegetable pastries, and mounds of queer, foreign Tartarean fruits, like kumquats and red bananas and black cherries, which were unfamiliar to the Amazon girl, but which Callipygia found delicious.

The hall itself, as I have said, was immense, with walls of rough stone and high ceilings held up by ancient, smoke-blackened rafters. The vast trestle table which ran the length of the hall had room enough on its strong benches for a hundred warriors and nobles and their ladies, and tonight every place was filled. The company drank toast after toast to Mandricardo and Callipygia, and, although the Amazon girl did not care for the Tartars' national drink (fermented mare's milk), or the fiery honey-mead they also drank, there was, she found to her relief, a large enough assortment of more conventional wines and champagnes to enable her to acknowledge each toast, at least with a polite sip.

The walls of the long hall were hung with the colossal stuffed and mounted heads of savage beasts, all of them trophies of the chase, for King Agricane, it seemed, was a famous huntsman, celebrated for his prowess in the pursuit of wild game far beyond the borders of his own kingdom. As Sir Malaprop put it in his inimitable way, the monarch was "a veritable Ramrod."*

Now, most of these stuffed and mounted heads were of fabulous beasts (or, at least, beasts that would seem purely fabulous to us who live here in Terra Cognita, the Lands We Know). It appeared that King Agricane scorned as suited only to effeminates and weaklings the hunting of mere ordinary, everyday lions or wild boar or panthers or the like, and devoted his huntsmanly skills to the pursuing and slaughter of creatures rarely glimpsed beyond the pages of the Bestiaries.

In this area of manly endeavor, of course, he and our old friend, Sir Malaprop, discovered a common interest. As soon as the Tartar monarch came to realize that his bald and red-faced little guest was none other than a *de Malaprop*, whose glorious doom and destiny it was to devote his days to hunting the elusive Galumphing Beast (of which there was only one, and no other of its kind had *ever* been slaughtered in the chase), he was filled with admiring questions. Flattered, and more than a little flustered by all this attention from the King, Sir Malaprop hemmed and hak-kaffed and did his best to describe the dear Beast and all of its quaint and curious little ways.

After a while, deep in a highly technical conversation, and arm and arm, the towering monarch and the stout little knight wandered out into the stables, where the grooms had tethered the famous Steed of Brass, so that Sir Malaprop could

---

* Of course, the dear little old knight meant "Nimrod," but never mind that. His auditors understood what he meant, anyway, and that's what matters in conversation.

show his host the fewmets, or droppings, of the
fabulously rare Beast, which were in his luggage.
Having eaten and drunk, until she felt certain that
she could no longer take aboard either a sip or a
morsel more, Callipygia pled the need for fresh
air, and left the vast hall. It was not so much fresh
air that she really needed, although that would be
nice, after all the smoke and the fumes of strong
drink and steaming platters of meat—the dinner-
feast was at the fowl course just then, and huge
dishes loaded with broiled peacocks stuffed with
nightingales, and grouse, pheasant and roast duck,
goose and wild turkey were being taken around
and around the long trestle table—as a little peace
and quiet.

It seems the wild and savage Tartars adore nothing more fervently than a good reason to throw a
party to celebrate in their own peculiar manner
some event or another. And that peculiar manner
they had of celebrating was given to dancing the
length of the table, kicking over wine goblets and
juggling burning torches or razor-sharp stilettos,
or leaping full across the table with wild and savage yells—and, as often as not, failing to quite
make it, and landing full on top of a benchful of
half-drunken, reveling feasters, which bench usually went over with a crash on the slate-tiled floor.

And then—there was the *music*. When they throw
a feast, the musicians of Tartary, it seemed, do
not saw decorously on violins, or pluck on the
strings of pretty lutes, or tootle melodiously on
flutes. No, not they! They give vent to lusty, roaring calls sounded through eight-foot-long horns,
designed to frighten off goblins and imps and
suchlike vermin; or boom and thump on huge
drums covered with the hides of leopards and so

big that men can (and do) dance upon them, and they also do their very best to drown out the roar of conversation and merriment by playing a wild and deafening music on curious Tartar instruments, half guitar and half zither, which make sounds that are louder than a cage full of furious wildcats.

Oh, for a little peace and quiet! thought Callipygia, as she slipped through the huge slab of hoary oak that served the castle as a door to the gardens. Out into the cool darkness and sweet moonlight she went, carefully closing the foot-thick door behind her. The roar and thunder of the merrymakers at their feast ceased abruptly, the moment the door was shut.

It was so nice out here among the moonlight roses; the air was fresh and invigorating, and the dark of night was a blessing, after the blaze of those huge fireplaces (they had just put the fish course on the spit, and were turning seven-foot-long salmon and trout and sturgeon and tuna over the sizzling bonfires) and from the ten thousand candles which also served to illuminate the air, which was so full of smoke and steam by this time, that it would have taken no fewer than ten thousand candles to do the trick.*

Thinking back over the noise and tumult and confusion of the feast, Callipygia sighed a little to herself.

---

* Of course, it is seriously to be doubted that the Amazon girl actually counted all of the candles which lit the feasting-hall—it would have taken her at least until noontime the next day, for that. Probably, King Agricane remarked to her on the number, or Mandricardo, perhaps. Incidentally, the *Chronicle Narrative* informs us that most of them (the candles, I mean) were as tall as a grown man and as big around as a man's upper thigh.

"My goodness," the girl murmured to the stars, "if they do all *that* just to say 'welcome home,' what do you suppose they'll do to celebrate our wedding?"

She shuddered slightly at the thought, unable to imagine any Tartarean excesses enormous and noisy enough . . .

"Hem?" inquired a voice from the patio. "Speakin' to me, m' dear?"

It was Sir Malaprop. The old knight was quaintly attired in a long nightgown, his rather stout form wrapped in a patched and worn bathrobe almost as old as he was. A dilapidated pair of carpet slippers were on his feet, and he had pulled a tasseled stocking-cap on his head to protect his hairless pate from the breezes and damps and chills of a Tartarean evening.

He reclined comfortably in the folding lawn chair which he had borrowed from Sir Braggadochio, and was puffing on a cigar between sips of ancient brandy from King Agricane's private cellar. He looked *very* comfortable.

"Oh, no," smiled Callipygia, seating herself on one of the rustic benches that were scattered about the garden terrace. "Just to myself . . . so hot and smoky and *noisy* in there, I just felt I had to get away and take a walk in the moonlight, before going to bed . . ."

"Quite," said the old knight. "Felt the same way, meself. Agricane is a delightful chap—hospitable to a fault!—and he certainly knows how to lay out a full table. But his guests, ker-hem!, methinks they leave something to be desired . . . a rather wild and ruffianly lot."

Callipygia sighed. "Yes . . . and it makes me

wonder how I'm going to *stand* having dinner every night in a smoky hall full of them, dancing on the table and juggling daggers and torches and so on, jumping over the tables—"

Sir Malaprop set down his cigar and the brandy glass and, removing his pair of tiny spectacles, began polishing them on a clean handkerchief he had worn tucked into the sleeve of his robe.

"Don't b'lieve you'll have any *problems* in that quarter, m' dear," he said confidentially. "While I was showin' the King the fewmets of the dear Beast—we were out in the stables, you know—the King told me that once you and your young man were spliced up all fit an' proper, he meant to give you a cozy little castle in the hills, where there were plenty of woods teeming with wild game for huntin' and a good trout stream for fishin' . . . and you were goin' to have the place all to yerselves, what, except for a half-dozen guards, some huntsmen, a butler and lady's maid, the cook and laundress and housekeeper, a few grooms and whatnot. Snug and cozy and secluded . . ." the old knight sounded wistful all of a sudden, ". . . certainly sounds quiet and peaceful and nice," he finished with a sigh.

"Then come and join us there," said Callipygia impulsively. "You and Sir Braggadochio can share it with us! You two can play checkers in front of the fire on wintry nights, when the furious gales of Tartary howl about the battlements and claw at the shutters . . . and go hunting when you care to, or fishing—"

"Always liked the idee of fishin'," the old knight admitted, dreamily. "Never had th' time fer it, meself. The Beast, you understand . . . always leading me into savage wildernesses and burnin' deserts and rocky gorges, and so on. Always wished I had the time to learn the knack o' fishin' . . ."

"Well, you'll have plenty of time to master that art, as our guest in the hills," said the Amazon girl.

The old knight heaved a sigh. "No chance of that, I'm afraid, m' dear! Must be up and about before very long, a-huntin' of th' Beast, you know. The Curse of the Malaprops they call it, and a curse it is, dash it all."

Suddenly, Callipygia got a brilliant idea.

"Tell me," she said, "when you're hunting this Galumphing Beast of yours, you're actually just wandering about where you will, aren't you? I mean, you don't *really* know just where the Beast actually is at the time, do you? It could be galumphing about a thousand leagues away and in the exact opposite direction from the one in which you are traveling, right?"

The knight cleared his breath. "Hem! Quite right, sorry to say, m'dear! Which is why I sometimes go *years* before spottin' the dear creature."

"Then," said Callipygia cunningly, "what would be the difference (since you only encounter your prey by sheer chance and pure accident) if you just stayed in one place, and waited for the Beast to come to *you?* Wouldn't the result be just the same? You'd have as much chance of the Beast happening to galumph by where you were, as you would out on the road hunting for it? Am I wrong?"

Sir Malaprop dropped his cigar. Then he straightened up in the folding lawn chair and his glasses fell off. He looked completely astonished, and, in fact, he was. For Callipygia's idea had never before occurred to him: and, of course, she was completely right.

"Well, hell's bones!" he ejaculated.

"And we'll see to it personally, Mandro and I, that you have the deepest and softest and coziest feather bed in this half of Asia, even if we have to have a magician steal it from the very bedroom of Prester John!"

"My, my," the old knight marvelled. "And would there be, you know, hem!, lots of little goosedown pillows, do you suppose?"

"Oodles and oodles of them," said the Amazon girl sweetly. "As many as you wish—dozens, in fact."

Sir Malaprop, like so many other men of action, was capable of reaching his decisions in life swiftly. He smacked one plump fist on the arm of the lawn chair.

"Then I'll just *do* it! Blankety-blanky blank-blank, if I don't! Like you say, the dear Beast is every bit as likely to come galumphing up to your snug little castle in th' woods, as anywhere else, by blankety-blank!"

Then, recollecting his emotional lapse into bad language, he colored, and added, "Haff! You'll have to par'm my Babylonian, ma'm!"

"You're par'med," said Callipygia, fondly.

Which leaves me with nothing further to add than the ancient and time-honored last line of tales such as this one has become, to wit:

And they all lived happily ever after!

E X P L I C I T

The Notes to Callipygia

CHAPTER ONE

Pontus, et al. As the story says, it was indeed
Herodotus who informs us that the famous country of the Amazons was situated in Pontus near
the Euxine Sea, and that its capital, Themiscyra,
rose on the shore of the river Thermodon.

I must presume that the Father of History
knew what he was talking about. Writing about,
I guess I mean.

Antiope, etc. The daughters of Queen Megamastaia,
for the most part, seemed to have been
named after some of their more distinguished
ancestresses. That is, "Antiope" and, of course,
"Hippolyta" are royal Amazons who figure prom-
inently in the histories of Hercules and Theseus.
"Kaydesa" is mentioned in one or another of
Swinburne's poems (I'm ashamed to say I forget
which poem). "Penthesileia" was the Queen of
the Amazons who took part in the final phase of

the Trojan War, while "Radigund" was an
Amazonian queen in Spenser's *Faerie Queene*. As
for "Emelye," she was the younger sister of
Queen Hippolyta—the one whom Theseus car-
ried off to Athens, you know. (Chaucer called
her "Ypolita," but never mind: in his day the
English language was still in a formative phase.)
She became a bone of contention between two
young Athenian knights, Sir Palamon and Sir
Arcite, and you can read all about it in the
Knight's Tale, in Chaucer's *Canterbury Tales.*

My notebooks are full of stuff like this.

CHAPTER TWO

Usquebae. The historians, or whatever you want to
call the experts on the history of making booze,
are not in agreement as to whether it was the
Irish or the Scots who invented the fine art of
brewing, blending and distilling whiskey, but it
was after the Romans, left, that's for sure. I feel
fairly certain that, to whomever the original
honor may belong, it must have been the Scots,
at least, who invented *Scotch* whiskey . . . which
was, of course, what Sir Braggadocio was drinking.

Busyrane. You will find something of the history of this enchanter in the *Faerie Queene,* an
invaluable treatise by the historian Spenser to
which, I rather fear, we will often refer in these
Notes.

Wandering Garden. Its actual name was "the Bower
of Bliss," and you can read all about it, and the
Enchantress Acrasia, in that admirable, if interminable, treatise, *The Faerie Queene,* by the historian Spenser.

Braggadocio. A treacherous and boastful coward who struts about in stolen armor in the pages of (yes, again) the *Faerie Queen*. I feel certain our Braggadocio is not Spenser's Braggadocio (for one thing, Spenser didn't mention his drinking problem, or that he talked in a broad Scots dialect, and he was usually scrupulously accurate on such details), but that doesn't mean they could not have been related.

CHAPTER THREE

Eriphilia, et al. The Amazonlike giantess appears in Spenser, as you by now have come to expect; the Siege of Albracca is recounted in the *Orlando Furioso*; Sans Foy, as well as his two brothers, Sans Joy and Sans Loy, were defeated by the Red Crosse Knight (St. George) in the *Faerie Queene*.

Rogero. Not only did he later become King of Bulgaria but also he was the founder of the famous House of d'Este.

Taprobane. Actually, this doesn't sound much like the Taprobane we visited in the first volume of this series, *Kesrick* (1982): could the historian who compiled the *Chronicle Narrative* have confused Serendib with Taprobane, I wonder? After all, one tropic isle is quite a lot like another, down there under Hindoostan.

Cephus, Tregelaphus, et cet. Cephus, Tregelaphus, Myrmecoles, Senad, Palmipeds and the Sadhuzag, are described in very much these same terms in the *Temptations of St. Antony* by Gustave Flaubert. This is a novel-length narrative in the form of a prose drama, and one of the richest

fantastic tales ever told, to the which I commend your attention. Among the characters
are the Buddha, Simon Magus, the god Zeus,
St. Anthony himself, Apollonius of Tyana, and
the Queen of Sheba—to say nothing of the
Devil.

Tregelaphus and the Sadhuzag. These two beasts are
particularly described, and in more detail than
above, in T. H. White's delicious *Book of Beasts,*
his translation of a Twelfth Century Latin besti-
ary, which I also commend to your attention.

Bunnassa, son of Busannas, etc. Very likely a scion of
the same ancient dynasty of the Taprobanian
monarchy to which also, and earlier, belonged
the King Nabussan, the son of Nassanub, the
grandson of Nabassun who figures so largely in
Voltaire's delightful and informative treatise,
Zadig, or Fate.

CHAPTER FOUR

Galumphing Beast, the. Although apparently hith-
erto unchronicled in the literature of chivalry,
this particular Best seems to be very much of a
kind with its more celebrated colleagues, or relatives, or whatever the word should be. I refer
to the Questing Beast which King Pellinore pursued in Malory's *Le Morte D'Arthur* (and also in
T. H. White's superlative history, *The Sword in
the Stone*) and the Blatant Beast hunted by
Sir Pelleas in the abovementioned treatise by
Spenser. The Blatant Beast was, Spenser informs us, "a dreadful fiend of gods and men
ydrad"; it was the spawn of Cerberus and the
Chimaera, and besides being hunted by Sir

Pelleas, Sir Calidore pursued the monster for awhile.

Spenser, incidentally, seems to have coined the word "blatant," perhaps from "blate," an obsolete word which means "to bellow." For that matter, it was the immortal Lewis Carroll who coined the word "galumphing," which you will find employed for the first time in literature in his poem "Jabberwocky."

Ah, those notebooks of mine. . . !

CHAPTER FIVE

Crysaor. You might well call him (her? it?) the "forgotten beast of Greek mythology," for, outside of being listed in Hesiod's *Theogony*, he is conspicuous in his absence from the Greek myths. For the purpose of my narrative, I have assumed him to be another winged horse like his more famous brother, Pegasus, but this is merely an assumption on my part.

CHAPTER SEVEN

Trolls. I am greatly indebted to the several works of the noted folklorist, scholar, and collector of traditional tales and fairy stories, Ruth Manning-Sanders, whose introductory material to her collection *A Book of Ogres and Trolls* (Dutton, 1973) points out that Trolls (perhaps because they are related to the Jotuns) prefer to dwell in the north, while Ogres like to live in the more southerly parts of Europe.

Miss Manning-Sanders also discusses the fact that, traditionally, Ogres live in dens, Trolls in caves, and Giants in castles. And who am I to refute her?

CHAPTER EIGHT

Cormoran, etc. These are all Giants famous in the
chronicles of Terra Magica. Cormoran himself,
who was a Cornish Giant and stood eighteen
feet tall and was three yards about, was the first
Giant to be slain by the celebrated Jack the
Giant-Killer. Jack dug a pit twenty-two feet deep
and tricked the dull-witted Giant into falling in,
then brained him with a pickaxe as he lay
stunned at the bottom. Not very sporting, I
suppose, but certainly effective.

Blunderbore, Jack's second kill, was the lord
of an enchanted castle amidst a lonely wood.
Jack strangled both Blunderbore and another
Giant, not named in the story, whom Blunderbore had invited to join him for dinner, with
Jack as the main course. Colbrand was a famous Danish Giant, slain by Guy of Warwick,
while you will read some little bit more about
the Giant of the Brazen Tower in *Don Quixote.*

CHAPTER NINE

Brazen Steed, the. According to the historian Chaucer, in his celebrated treatise *The Squire's Tale,*
the magically-animated clockwork Horse bore
the Knight of the Mirror all the way to the
Court of Cambuscan, the Emperor of Tartary,
bearing with him a love-letter addressed to
Cambuscan's daughter, the Princess Canace, as
well as certain magical gifts. As I have already
described these gifts in the text of this chapter,
there seems no need to repeat myself here. But
I have always wondered about that "language of
the birds" stuff, myself.

Chaucer tells us that the Knight of the Mirror

was dispatched by the Grand Prince of the Indies (well, actually, he said the "kyng of Arabie and of Inde," but never mind), with a proposal for the hand of the Princess from that monarch. Rather annoyingly, Chaucer never bothered to complete this particular narrative in the *Canterbury Tales*, so we will never know how things came out in the end.

CHAPTER TEN

Aptly-named. That is, the name of Sir Blundamore's snow-white charger, Blanc-Neige, *means* "Snow-White" in French.

CHAPTER ELEVEN

Smith & Tinker. A distinguished firm of magical inventors who formerly flourished in the Land of Ev, more or less, and later relocated (for some reason which I forget) to the interior of the Moon. They are best known for having designed and built the celebrated Clockwork Man, Tik-Tok, who can move, think and speak and do everything but live. You can read all about him, of course, in the Oz books of L. Frank Baum.

CHAPTER TWELVE

Sangaranga. That most loquacious of all celebrated explorers, Sir John de Mandeville, informs us, in his *Voyages and Travels,* that the kingdom of Sangaranga is "very much plagued and tormented by sorcerers." As usual, Sir John seems to have hit the nail on the head.

CHAPTER THIRTEEN

Always had a head for history. That is to say, the Queen of Sangaranga named her daughter after Princess Angelica of China, the noted heroine of the *Orlando Furioso* ... which, you will remember, is a sober historical work in Terra Magica, although an extravagant chivalric romance in our own world.

CHAPTER SEVENTEEN

Angelica F. As I have elsewhere noted in the course of this series, I am indebted to the historian Milne, who, in his admirable treatise, *Once On a Time,* informs us that this is the manner in which princesses in magical countries are accustomed to sign their names. (The "F.", by the way, stands for *Fecit.*)

CHAPTER NINETEEN

Riches of Creosote. Of course, the old fellow meant to say "riches of Croesus," but they don't call him "Malaprop" for nothing, you know.

CHAPTER TWENTY-ONE

The Fairy Blackstick. This personage is discussed at much greater length in a work by the historian Thackeray called *The Rose and the Ring.* By a pretty coincidence, which I have only just now noticed, in that work she *also* serves as Fairy Godmother to a princess named Angelica.

CHAPTER TWENTY-TWO

Femenye. In his account of Sir Palamon of Athens and his fellow-knight (and also cousin) Sir Arcite, which tells of their contention for the love of the Amazonian princess, Emelye, in the *Knight's Tale,* Chaucer apparently confuses the two countries of Amazonia and Femenye, and uses the two names interchangeably. Sir John de Mandeville, on the other hand, in his *Travels and Voyages,* correctly distinguished between Amazonia, which is situated in Pontus on the Black Sea, and Femenye, which is to be found in the remoter parts of Asia.

Of the two opinions, I have to go along with Sir John's. I mean—after all, he was *there.*

CHAPTER TWENTY-FOUR

Aeskja Hrinja. It would seem likely that Trollish is closely similar to Old Icelandic; at least *aeskja-hrinja* means "wish-ring" in Icelandic.

Zzzzyytpk. This world of transformation in Troll Magic may be found in the old Danish folktale "The Troll's Little Daughter," and I am indebted to Ruth Manning-Sanders, in her *Book of Ogres and Trolls* for drawing it to my attention. According to that story, you pronounce the word forward to change the form of something, and pronounce it backward to undo the transformation—and if you can say "*zzzzyytpk*" either forward *or* backward, by golly, you've got a more nimble tongue than I have!

Incidentally, this may possibly be the same magic wishing ring the Troll gave his daughter in the Icelandic tale, "Sigurd the King's Son."

The End of the Notes to *Callipygia*

DAW

THE SPECIAL MAGIC OF
ANDRE NORTON

Andre Norton is one of the foremost names in the world of fantasy and science fiction. Here is high adventure on other worlds and in other dimensions, from the hands of a master storyteller.

THE WITCH WORLD NOVELS
- ☐ SPELL OF THE WITCH WORLD   (UE2242—$3.50)
- ☐ LORE OF THE WITCH WORLD   (UE2243—$3.50)
- ☐ HORN CROWN   (UE2051—$2.95)

OTHER TITLES
- ☐ THE BOOK OF ANDRE NORTON   (UE2247—$2.95)
- ☐ GARAN THE ETERNAL   (UE2244—$2.95)
- ☐ MERLIN'S MIRROR   (UE2245—$2.95)
- ☐ PERILOUS DREAMS   (UE2248—$2.95)
- ☐ QUAG KEEP   (UE2250—$2.95)
- ☐ YURTH BURDEN   (UE2249—$2.95)

DAW

A Writer of Epic Fantasy in the Grand Tradition

Peter Morwood

THE BOOK OF YEARS

☐ **THE HORSE LORD: Book 1**   (UE2178—$3.50)

Centuries ago, the Horse Lords had ridden into Alba to defeat an evil sorcerer and banish magic from the land. Now an ambitious lord has meddled with dark forces, and the ancient evil is unleashed again. Rescued by an aging wizard, young Aldric seeks revenge on the sorcerous foe who has slain his clan and stolen his birthright.

☐ **THE DEMON LORD: Book 2**   (UE2204—$3.50)

Aldric must undertake a secret mission that will lead him to the troubled border provinces. There he finds unexpected allies: a mysterious, not-quite-trustworthy Demon Queller, and the beautiful young heir to a demon-possessed citadel. Together, they journey to the fortress of Seghar to challenge the demon spirit that holds it in its wrathful grasp.

☐ **THE DRAGON LORD: Book 3**   (UE2252—$3.50)

As a warrior's honor leads Aldric into the heart of the Drusalan Empire on the king's orders, unbeknownst to him, the king has betrayed him into enemy hands. Slowly the trap closes about him, while powerful allies are riding to his aid: the wizard Gemmel and the mighty warrior Dewan. But can even they help Aldric against dark and deadly sorcery and a monstrous dragon?

DAW

MAGIC TALES FROM THE MASTERS OF FANTASY

- [ ] **MARION ZIMMER BRADLEY, Lythande** (UE2154—$3.50)
- [ ] **LIN CARTER, Mandricardo** (UE2180—$2.95)
- [ ] **C.J. CHERRYH, The Dreamstone** (UE2013—$2.95)
  The Tree of Swords and
  Jewels (UE1850—$2.95)
- [ ] **JO CLAYTON, Drinker of Souls** (UE2123—$3.50)
- [ ] **B.W. CLOUGH, The Dragon of Mishbil** (UE2078—$2.95)
- [ ] **SHARON GREEN, The Far Side of Forever**
  (UE2212—$3.50)
- [ ] **MERCEDES LACKEY, Arrows of the**
  Queen (UE2189—$2.95)
  Arrow's Flight (UE2222—$3.50)
- [ ] **MICHAEL MOORCOCK, Elric at the End of Time**
  (UE2228—$3.50)
- [ ] **PETER MORWOOD, The Horse Lord** (UE2178—$3.50)
  The Demon Lord (UE2204—$3.50)
- [ ] **ANDRE NORTON, Spell of the Witch World**
  (UE2242—$3.50)
- [ ] **JENNIFER ROBERSON, Sword-Dancer** (UE2152—$3.50)
- [ ] **MICHAEL SHEA, Nifft the Lean** (UE1783—$2.95)
- [ ] **TAD WILLIAMS, Tailchaser's Song** (UE2162—$3.95)

Write for free DAW catalog of hundreds of other titles!
(Prices slightly higher in Canada.)

NEW AMERICAN LIBRARY
P.O. Box 999, Bergenfield, New Jersey 07621

Please send me the DAW BOOKS I have checked above. I am enclosing $_____
(check or money order—no currency or C.O.D.'s). Please include the list price plus
$1.00 per order to cover handling costs. Prices and numbers are subject to change
without notice.

Name _____

Address _____

City _____ State _____ Zip _____

Please allow 4-6 weeks for delivery.